From the Edge

Lori Bell

Cover photograph by CanStock Photo

Printed by CreateSpace

ISBN 978 1717308153

DEDICATION

To tried and true friends.
There are fewer gifts in life that are more special.

Chapter One

The bar was half full of people. A sparse crowd in the middle of the week was to be expected. Three shot glasses of tequila were placed on the table between them. Carrie tipped hers to her mouth and sipped it almost too slowly, or timidly. Tabitha tossed hers back in one swallow. The third glass remained untouched.

Tabitha made the first move to pick it up with her thumb and index finger. She raised it momentarily. "To Beth. Happy 40th!" She was careful to only drink half. And then offered the rest to Carrie. As Carrie took it, her eyes clouded with tears. She didn't want to be the one to cry. *Why was Tabitha always the stronger one?* She raised the tiny glass. "We love you, Bethie."

All three of the glasses sat empty on their table, as the friends for more than two decades shared a comfortable silence. Carrie traced the rim of one of the shot glasses with her finger, and Tabitha watched her. Tabitha was, on the exterior, the one who always appeared entirely put together. Her caramel-colored long hair reached her shoulders. She had used a flat iron tonight. Carrie wondered how she had the time to give such attention to herself. Tabitha was an emergency room nurse, often working twelve hour days, and then going home to her husband and sons. And still, Tabitha had manicured nails, not a single visible gray hair on her head, and a body with the same toned muscles and curves that she had in college. Maybe she had gone from a size six to an eight, but it was unnoticeable. Tabitha and Carrie were not always close in an inseparable, deeply connected, kind of way. It was Beth who brought the three of them together, recognizing and solidifying their bond. She somehow always had been able to make their friendship effortless, beginning twenty-plus years ago in college when the three of them first met. Tabitha was wild, Carrie was the better-safe-than-sorry one, and Beth was placed evenly between the two. Beth claimed she was designed the best. She avoided trouble (unlike Tabitha), but tempted fate and sought out fun (unlike Carrie).

Tabitha reached for Carrie's hand, taking her attention away from fingering the empty miniature glass. She held it, as their eyes met. "It's okay to talk about it. We have, I know, but we've also somehow transitioned to dancing around it, as if not mentioning it makes it go away." Tabitha was also the say-it-like-it-was, straightforward one.

"It's never going to *go away*," Carrie finally spoke. She was capable of speaking her mind, too. Or maybe Tabitha brought that out of her.

Tabitha nodded in agreement. "And it also seems like it will not get any easier than it feels right now." Carrie heard Tabitha's every word, and squeezed her hand tighter. *She understood.* They were connected on a deeper level now because of their shared pain. That's why, in the last several months, they turned to each other more than ever throughout the history of their friendship.

Tabitha noticed and traced her finger on the fine streak of dull gray paint which stained the edge of Carrie's thumb. "Painting again? How's that going for you?"

Carrie smiled. She had missed a spot when she washed her hands. Traces of her hobby-turned-fulltime-career were always present. "Not much inspiration, but I've taken the advice of a good friend and I'm putting something down on canvas daily." That *good friend* was Tabitha, when she had warned Carrie not to lose herself. *Keep at it. I don't care if you paint a house on a dinner napkin, just do something every single day to keep your creativity alive and flowing.*

Carrie failed to mention that all she had managed to brush on canvas was dark and drab. Nothing at all like the sunshine and rainbows, so to speak, in every bright and cheery piece of artwork that once hung on canvas on the walls of their apartment the three of them shared in college. Her older paintings were still selling online and straight from her gallery in Hays, Kansas. The occasional request from patrons for something new was heard, but Carrie just wasn't able to deliver lately.

"Good." Tabitha smiled, and let go of Carrie's hand. An unruly blonde curl fell over her left eye, and Carrie brushed it away. She had loose, big curls all over her head. *Oh this hair,* Carrie wanted to say, as it had always been defiant to anything new or different that she wanted to try. She also wanted to curse the muffin top she felt melting over the tight waistband of her dark-washed denim tonight. Her blouse had not been blousy enough. She felt how it molded to her stomach roll. How many times in the last several years had she said she wanted to, needed to, lose ten or fifteen pounds? Truth be told, it never bothered her in her youth, or in college, as much as it disturbed her as an adult. Seeing how Tabitha successfully stayed in shape didn't help. It actually unnerved her. "How about another drink?" Tabitha interrupted Carrie's insecure thoughts. "Should we continue with tequila, and order margaritas?"

"One more," Carrie suggested in reply, and the two of them laughed in unison. That was Beth's line. She always used to say, one more, and they knew all too well there was no such thing as just one more.

Over an hour later, they both probably had one too many, but the alcohol was both freeing and comforting. They had so easily fallen into talking about their current lives, as well as the times they shared throughout their college years. *Memories.* The bar had emptied out a little, so it was more noticeable when the door opened and someone came in. Carrie was within view of the entrance, and she had seen him first. "Don't turn around," her face flushed as she spoke. *And why was it that every time someone said 'don't turn around,' the other person always turned around?*

"Holy shit…" Tabitha said, whipping her head back around to face Carrie again. "This can't be happening. Seriously? Tonight of all nights? I'm just drunk enough to cause a scene, you know."

Carrie immediately reached across the table for Tabitha's hand. She wasn't gentle. She held tight, and reached even higher up at her wrist. "Don't think that I do not feel exactly the same, but no, you will not go over there. Keep sitting. He didn't see us." Carrie moved only her eyes to watch Joe Morgan sit down on a stool at the end of the bar. His back was now to them.

Tall, broad shoulders, jet-black hair. *Arrogant* was written all over that man. *Son of a bitch* was, too.

"How long has it been since you've seen him around Hays?" Tabitha asked, as if it really mattered. Never seeing him again would have been too soon for the both of them.

"The last time I saw him was the last time you saw him." Tabitha knew exactly what Carrie meant. And then they both couldn't help but think about how they initially met Joe Morgan. Beth had introduced them. She was head over heels, ridiculously in love — or infatuated — with him. Neither Tabitha nor Carrie had ever seen her so caught up in a man. And they had all three been through their share of love, lust, and heartbreak in college. But this was years after they had attended Fort Hays State University together. They were adults, out in the working world, dealing with real life and families. Except for Beth. She had yet to find love. She married too young. She was the first of the three of them to say I do, and then, I don't. Following her divorce, being married less than one year, Beth claimed not to be in a hurry. And she wasn't for quite awhile. But then she reached her mid thirties and she most definitely was hell-bent to finally find the one. She wanted a husband — someone to share her life with, and have babies. She was running out of time. But time had stood still when Joe Morgan waltzed into her world. And then all she wanted was him.

"I can't sit here. We are not staying here." Tabitha was adamant, and when she made an attempt to reach for her handbag on the chair beside her, Carrie stopped her.

"No. We still need to chase this tequila down with a couple of glasses of water. Neither one of us is driving anytime soon." Carrie watched Tabitha frown at her, and the lines on her forehead stayed visible. Wrinkles. The skin's response to Father Time. At forty, they were already succumbing to aging.

Tabitha obliged, but she wasn't at all happy about it. "Fuck you," she scoffed. It's what they did. It was their history. She didn't honestly mean the inappropriate, harsh words. Carrie saw how Tabitha's mouth twitched into a crooked smile, and the hint of laughter that danced in her eyes.

"No, fuck him, for what he did to all of our lives." Carrie tipped back the last of her drink, and chewed on a lone chunk of ice in her mouth, while Tabitha watched her and wished her own glass had not already been empty. This was the Carrie she remembered surfacing from time to time that Tabitha was drawn to. She sometimes allowed herself to consume too much alcohol and didn't shy away from cursing. Still, Carrie ultimately was the one with the level head. Her intention now was to stay put and not escape being in the same place at the same time as Joe Morgan. They wouldn't allow his presence to chase them away. But Tabitha sensed this night was not going to end well.

Chapter Two

Tabitha stepped away from their table to use the restroom. Carrie also had the overwhelming urge to pee, but she waited. Luckily, the restroom was located in the opposite direction of the bar, where Joe Morgan was still perched on an end stool. Carrie could just imagine Tabitha passing him, his back still to her and oblivious to what was about to hit him. *Literally.* He deserved more than a fist, or a drink, in his face.

Carrie imagined painting a scene right now. It caught her off guard, as she had not been inspired for several months. But this wasn't an image she would share with the world. This was just something that, at the moment, took up space in her mind. A man, broad shouldered, dark hair, dark eyes, dark clothing. Standing in the distance, his back to the scene. Underneath the night sky on a lone street, where only a pole light shone. And in the forefront was Beth. Dark brown (almost black) hair, fair skin, the bluest eyes. She stood with a turned stance partially in the direction of the man in the distance. Torn. Torn for which way to turn. *To him. Or to reality.* Joe Morgan was a fantasy for Beth. He never was who she believed him to be. And she should have left him in dreamland. He didn't belong in her world. He was never worthy of kindhearted Beth.

"You're staring," Tabitha spoke as she sat back down at their table, with a now empty bladder. Carrie needed that feeling of relief, too.

"I'm painting in my mind," Carrie admitted.

"Him?" Tabitha gave her a look of disapproval. Carrie nodded. "Well set fire to that canvas when you're through. He deserves to burn in hell."

Carrie giggled, and then stood up to feel the immediate overflow of pee swooshing around in her bladder. There wasn't room for a drop more.

It was Tabitha's turn to stare. She practically had to spin her head entirely around to be in direct view of the bar. *What was he doing there? Besides the obvious. And really, why did he have to choose that bar, of all the bars in Hays, tonight!* Tabitha stood up abruptly from the table. She had her wristlet in one hand and their bar bill in the other. *Now was as good of a time as any to pay the bartender.*

She walked steadily in her heeled booties. One foot in front of the other until she felt someone come up behind her. Carrie slipped her arm through the loophole of Tabitha's and spun her back around. "Let's go," Tabitha heard the adamancy in her tone. Her grip on her arm was seriously firm too.

With their arms still hooked, they made their way through the bar, en route to the exit. The bartender caught Carrie's eye and she spoke to him. "Cash on the table, Harry. We're leaving."

"Thank you, ladies!" Harry's voice carried throughout the bar, and when they both turned their heads to acknowledge him, Joe Morgan was staring directly at them.

The door slammed behind Carrie after she practically pushed Tabitha through it. "Did you see how he was looking at us?" was the first thing Tabitha said when they were alone in the warm, windy, outside air.

"I tried not to. I immediately looked away," Carrie stated. "I just can't. I don't know if I'll ever be able to stand the sight of him. And why should either of us be expected to?" Carrie's loose curls were blowing all over the place, and in her face. She used both of her hands to calm her disheveled hair.

"I stared the fucker down," Tabitha admitted, still feeling the anger that had risen in her chest inside of that bar. She didn't even attempt to fight the way the wind was whipping her own hair around.

"That's why I was escorting your ass out of there," Carrie attempted to suppress a grin, but failed.

"What are you a bouncer now?" Tabitha partly scoffed.

"Nope. Just protecting someone I love. He's not worth it, Tab."

"And how many times didn't we tell Beth exactly that?" Tabitha responded. She almost wished for another drink in her hand. Apparently there still wasn't enough alcohol in her system to numb the pain. Or to erase all of the hate.

"Not enough," Carrie stated, regretfully.

"Bullshit. An audio recording on repetitive play would not have gotten through to her. We have to accept that." Tabitha felt hot tears well up in her eyes, and she fought them, but not before Carrie noticed. Sometimes Tabitha did things that humanized herself, but only those closest to her were given those honest glimpses.

"We do have to accept it, but it just hurts too much still." Carrie's honesty was raw, as she reached for Tabitha, and they fell into an embrace that felt more like one was desperately trying to hold the other up. But that's what friends were for.

Carrie walked into a dark house. All she saw were the dim stair lights on each individual step of the full staircase that led to the second level. The steps were hardwood with a strip of off-white, tight ribbed, textured carpet embedded down the middle. She slipped off her ballet flats and kicked them aside before she reached the stairs. She was going straight to bed. It didn't matter if there were dishes in the sink or lunches to be packed for her children tomorrow. It could all wait until morning. This day was done.

One by one, Carrie peeked into the bedrooms of her eleven-year-old twin daughters. It was just last month when they no longer wanted to share the same bedroom. They were now directly across the hallway from each other. Close enough, they had told their mother, but it saddened Carrie to see them growing up and needing their own space. It was late, a quarter to one in the morning. Carrie was relieved to find their phones and other devices at rest, as they were. Living with preteens meant ever-changing rules, primarily because they were always trying to get by with something, and they for sure pushed their limits.

She padded the length of the hardwood hallway upstairs in her bare feet before she reached the master bedroom at the very end that she shared with her husband. She closed the door behind her, and then made her way through the room in the dark. She unbuttoned her blouse and peeled off her jeans. It was instant relief for her to be out of the snug denim. Her clothes were piled on the floor at the foot end of the bed when Carrie slipped between the sheets on her side of the mattress, still wearing her bra and panties. She lay there, realizing she needed to get back up and brush her teeth, wash the makeup from her face. And probably pee again. But her body was spent, so she didn't make the effort to move. The lump in the bed beside her never stirred. Gone were the days when they waited up for each other, because neither could fall asleep without the other beside them.

They had a sizeable house, two healthy girls, and a bank account that would never leave them wanting for anything. Carrie's successful painting career had not carried them financially. It was her husband's profession as an investment analyst for which the compensation was generous. On the outside, their lives looked nothing short of perfect. But if she had a choice, looking back to when they were first married with two babies at once and struggling to make ends meet in their mediocre income world, Carrie would choose to rewind time. She had changed too, she knew. She was older. Set in her ways. More responsible than fun. It wasn't all Dom.

Dominic Tyler, Carrie's husband of fifteen years, was sound asleep beside her. He was almost out of reach in their massive king-size bed. Who was she trying to fool? He *was* out of reach to her.

Unlike Carrie, Tabitha made her way home but did not immediately fall into bed. Sleep was the farthest thing on her radar. Her mind was reeling still. Dwelling on the fact that they came face to face with Joe Morgan tonight. *That man had a lot of balls to even remain in Hays, much less strut around town like people owed him something.* Tabitha retrieved an open bottle of white wine from the refrigerator, and she poured herself a full glass. The alcoholic mix of tequila and wine in her system wasn't going to be good for the hangover headache she already felt coming on. She drank it anyway.

She sat slightly slumped on a stool with her elbows on the countertop of the kitchen island. There was only a dim light on above the corner sink. Tabitha and her family lived in a modest, ranch-style, brick home in a safe, friendly neighborhood. They diligently kept up with remodels and upgrades, inside and out. It was hardly a home as extravagant as Carrie's mansion on the hill, but Tabitha loved the simplicity of it. On the exterior, she was a woman of high maintenance. Hair, nails, clothing, and keeping her body in shape. But her home wasn't flashy or showy. It was comfortable and lived-in. And it was one of her most favorite possessions in her world.

"Tab?" She must have dozed off after she finished her glass of wine. Her head was down, resting in the crook of her arm on the island's countertop. Her feet, one with a heeled bootie and one without, were dangling. Tingling too. All of her had apparently fallen asleep. She awoke to her husband's voice as he entered the still-dark kitchen. "Why don't you come to bed?"

She peeled her eyes. They felt dry and sticky. Her eyeballs burned. Those contacts in them weren't the ones made safe to leave in while sleeping. "Uh, yeah, I meant to. What time is it?"

"Three." Tabitha watched her husband take her empty wine glass off the counter in front of her. He rinsed the glass underneath the faucet in the sink, and then placed it upside down in the dishwasher. He was like that. He was for sure that kind of man. When there were things to be done, he did them. Without complaint. Without obligation. He physically took care of her, their boys, and the house they all lived in together. Rory

Chance was her husband of twelve years, and they were raising sons, twelve and nine years old.

Tabitha stood up, and then reached down to take off her one shoe. She had no idea where the other one was at the moment. "Come on, Cinderella," Rory placed his arm low around her waist. He was bare-chested, only wearing blue plaid pajama bottoms. Like Tabitha, he was in good shape at forty-years old. Tabitha smiled at his tousled brown hair. Bedhead. She assumed he and the boys had been tucked in and asleep for hours before she made it home.

"You've got tequila coming out of your pores," he pinched his nostrils closed to block the apparent stench coming from her body, as they walked to their bedroom together. She giggled. Tabitha preferred a daily glass of wine, but tonight she and Carrie had a special reason to indulge in tequila. It was Beth's favorite in college, and thereafter.

Tabitha fell onto their queen-size bed fully dressed. It felt good to lay her head down on her own firm pillow. She immediately closed her eyes, but then she felt Rory wrestling her out of her pants. He left her underwear on, but not without teasing her with his fingers. "Oh God, not now," Tabitha whined. And then she felt him slip off her sweater, arms and shoulders first, head last. He pinched both of her nipples through her bra.

"Horny fucker," she spoke, and laughed.

"I'll get you later," Rory whispered as he pressed his lips to hers and then pulled up the sheet and duvet to cover her underwear-clad body.

"Mmm, hmm…" was Tabitha's last response before she drifted off to slumber. She had exactly three hours before another twelve-hour shift in the ER. She worked ridiculously hard to keep her family afloat. Maybe today would be the day that Rory would get serious about his job search. His unemployment status was getting tiresome, and taking its toll. On her.

Chapter Three

The windshield wipers on Carrie's SUV, one of those full-size black vehicles like someone as significant as the President of the United States rode up in, were on full blast. The rain was coming down sideways, courtesy of the strong Kansas wind. Rain or shine, it was always windy in Hays. Carrie recalled the time she was moving into their newest home with Dom and their daughters. The twins were toddlers and one of them had left the car door open on the driveway. Later, Carrie discovered the door had been stretched off the hinges from the blusterous wind. She repeatedly used that example in story form whenever she wanted to sum up the extreme windy conditions in Kansas.

The rain was front and center on her mind this morning as she drove downtown to her art gallery. The last time she remembered it pouring like this, where she struggled to see past the windshield in front of her, was that night —just several months ago— when she and Tabitha received the same text message from Beth. *I want you both here.*

It was storming. They had both separately tried to call Beth back. She never picked up. They, in turn, called each other. Both had a cell phone pressed to an ear while they drove frantically and too fast.

She's not answering! (Carrie)

Go to her place! (Tabitha)

I know she's there! (Carrie)

This can't be good! (Carrie)

Dammit! (Tabitha)

Fucking rain! (Tabitha)

Hurry! (Carrie)

I am! (Tabitha)

The back and forth words of panic shared between Carrie and Tabitha were frozen in Carrie's memory. *How many times had she rehashed it? Too damn many. And it was pointless to dwell. But yet, she did.*

It was something entirely more evident and unmistakable than perfect timing when they both tore into the parking lot from opposite directions at the same time. Carrie came straight from her gallery where she had been painting late. She had gone back there to work after dinner, which she often did. Tabitha drove directly from home. She had already been headed to bed, after working another twelve-hour shift and preparing to do it all over again the following day. She had thrown on the pair of navy blue scrubs that were hanging on the back of her bedroom door for the morning. Carrie could still see the blood saturated across the chest of those scrubs soon after they arrived. She squeezed her eyes shut momentarily, hoping to push away the vision of that memory. Her windshield wipers were on full blast but the rain had tapered off some. The blades continued to move crazily in front of her. *Back and forth. Back and forth.* Carrie slowed the motion of them. She had tears on her face now. And for the rest of her morning drive, she allowed herself to remember again.

When Tabitha turned her vehicle in front of Carrie's, she raced into the parking lot of Beth's apartment building. Always the rebel, the rule-breaker, the one who never cared what other people thought. Tabitha parked sideways, directly in front of the complex, ignoring all of the strategically angled white lines designated for parking spaces. She assumed the role of an emergency vehicle. Well, in a way, that's what they both were there for. *To help Beth. To save Beth. To rescue Beth. Beth needed them for God's sake!* Carrie followed and didn't hesitate to park in the same reckless, emergent manner as Tabitha. Car doors were slammed and the two of them were still on the move when they met each other underneath a dark, stormy sky.

Tabitha had the lead, up the stairway, which was partially under cover from the rain that was still steadily coming down. She was taking two of those outdoor-carpeted steps at a time, and Carrie's adrenaline must have been in overdrive, because she was far from in-shape but almost on the heels of Tabitha's boat shoes, which she wore barefoot. When they reached the landing in front of apartment number nine, the door to Beth's place was standing wide open. She had known they would come as soon as they could. Of course they would. That's what those kinds of friends did. That's what this trio for more than two decades promised each other, for life. *We will be there. No matter what.*

Now, two blocks away from her destination at the gallery, the text tone from her cell phone startled her back to reality. Carrie looked down at her phone resting in the cup holder between the seats, and she read the message, visible on the home screen.

I never used to hate rainstorms.

It was from Tabitha. She was already a few hours into her shift at the hospital and had taken a break to stand in front of the window and peer out as the merciless rain splashed up against the glass.

I know the feeling. Carrie replied.

Tabitha was called away from the window. A gunshot victim had been brought into the emergency room. It was broad daylight. A husband apparently had accidentally shot his wife. He claimed to have been cleaning his gun. Tabitha heard the frantic calls after his wife, who was strapped to a gurney. Unconscious. Everything, her clothes, hair, skin, was saturated in blood. He called her name repeatedly, until someone tended to his hysterics as they rushed his wife away. *Elizabeth! Elizabeth!* Tabitha momentarily squeezed her eyes shut. She saw blood every single day. It wasn't that. It was the memory. Her name.

Less than thirty minutes later, Tabitha, who had aided the doctor's every move to try to stop the bleeding and stabilize the patient, watched him stop. He shook his head. He pulled off his bloody gloves, one by one. *There was nothing more they could do.*

She watched the doctor solemnly walk out of the room. Tabitha found a far corner, and pushed her back up against it, and eventually she slid down to the floor, on her bottom.

"Tabitha Chance? You okay?" Someone from the emergency room's medical team called out to her in the aftermath of what happened in hospitals every single day. Lives were lost.

"I am. I just need a minute." Her reply was definite. Her voice was strong. So everyone looked away. Tabitha pulled her knees up to her chest, and stared at her feet on the vinyl tiled flooring. Her navy blue clogs had blood splattered toes.

Her mind went to that night. She and Carrie had lunged their way through the doorway of Beth's apartment to find her lying on the floor between the kitchen and living room. Flat on her back, with a butcher knife protruding from her chest. *For the love of God! Her heart!* It was like living in a bad dream. A freaking nightmare. The sight was beyond surreal. While Tabitha had seen it all working in the ER, this was too damn much. Not to mention too close to home. Beth was family. And now Tabitha feared that she had harmed herself beyond saving. Considering her training and experience as a nurse, Tabitha knew how dire this looked. And she was frantic and worried with every fiber of her being.

There was screaming, panic, shock, and disbelief. *What in the hell were they seeing?* Tabitha remembered her and Carrie falling down to their knees, at Beth's side, as close as they could get to her. Tabitha sprung into action. She had to be a trauma nurse first. She had to save her. It's what she did. It's what she would do!

"Stay with us, Beth!" It wasn't a request. It was a demand. Her breathing was already too shallow. The blood loss was immense. There were multiple chest wounds, Tabitha concluded, and cringed at the thought of it taking Beth more than one try to stab on point. Carrie was holding onto Beth. Her hands. Her face. Carrie was the human being with real emotions in the room. She sobbed and begged for her to hold on. She wanted the knife removed from her chest, but Tabitha — who was in complete medical mode — warned her that would do so much more harm than good. The blade, in place, could be preventing major leakage from a cut vessel.

"Just save her!" Carrie had screamed.

Those words, just save her, still haunted Tabitha today. Tabitha had known exactly what Beth did to herself. She pierced her own heart. It was twisted, and sick, and utterly unbelievable. And she did it because she didn't want to be saved.

"She doesn't have long." Tabitha could still hear herself saying those words. She hated herself for having to speak it. She felt defeated. The paramedics were on their way. They would also make a desperate attempt to stabilize Beth. But no two people on this earth were more desperate for her survival than Tabitha and Carrie.

"What? No, no, no!" Carrie reacted. *"Bethie, Bethie! Look at us! You open those beautiful baby blues and look at us! Oh God, please. Please don't take her."*

"Stop…" Tabitha choked on her words. She didn't really mean it. She had to say it. This was it. Beth's last moments with them were at hand. She was dying in their arms. *"Just rest."* Beth needed to finally find peace.

Carrie wanted to shove Tabitha out of the way. She was encouraging their best friend to give up. To die. But reality sunk in quickly, and Carrie complied, pushing aside the shock that was rippling through her body. *"We love you so much,"* Her hands were shaking as she placed both of them on the face of their best friend. She unintentionally left bloody prints on her pale flesh. *"God, why did you do this to yourself?"*

Tabitha shook her head no, fiercely back and forth. *"No, Carrie. Don't."* Now was not the time. There was no more time. This was goodbye. *"We have to say goodbye."*

A torturous, god-awful goodbye. The three of them would no longer be a trio. One less made for them to never be the same. And yes, Carrie had said it aloud to Beth. *Why did you do this to yourself?* They knew why. And both of them were certain it was the saddest damn thing they would ever experience in their lifetimes. Beth couldn't handle heartbreak, so she purposely ended her life, with a blade through her own heart. It was like a Shakespearean novel at its worst. And while Beth's pain would now end, both Carrie and Tabitha were just beginning their agonizing struggle of loss. And disappointment.

They each held one of Beth's hands in their own. Their faces were wet with tears, and their throats were choked with sobs, and then Beth was gone.

Tabitha willed herself not to cry. She was working. She was a professional in a medical environment. She had a moment —sparked by what just happened to a patient in the ER, still lifeless on that gurney right now— where she needed to sink down to the floor and remember. She didn't belong down there though, not here and not now, she told herself as she rose to her feet and carried on.

Chapter Four

Carrie's thoughts were in sync with Tabitha's today, as she was in her studio in the back room of the gallery. Her feet were planted in front of a blank canvas, propped upright on an easel, and she was holding a dripping paint brush. She thought about the days and weeks following Beth's death, and how angry she had been with Tabitha. If Tabitha had allowed for them to encourage Beth to hold on, to fight for her life, maybe she would still be alive. It took Carrie months to realize she had directed all of her anger at Tabitha. Even her anger she had festered toward Beth. For giving up. For not crying out for help from the edge.

The two of them finally had a fallout over Beth's suicide. And that ironically was what brought them back together. They had come to a realization and finally a mutual understanding in the midst of their anger, and their hurtful, unretractable words. It was a moment of *we* are not to blame. *We are lashing out at each other for a choice that Beth made.* The woman, the friend, who brought them together in the very beginning on a campus full of strangers was the same person who nearly severed their bond forever. And that was the conversation Carrie now allowed herself to relive. It was a memory that took place in the studio where she stood at the moment.

"She wanted us both there." Carrie remembered having her back turned to the doorway in the studio. She had not heard anyone come in. It was no surprise, as she had been walking around for weeks in a fog. Her world had come to an abrupt, confusing and painfully sad halt, while the rest of the world went on. Without her. As if all was well. Before she even turned around, she knew that voice.

"What are you doing, Tabitha?" Carrie referred to both her presence there and her need to speak of Beth again.

"Reminding you that Beth wanted us both there. She didn't want to die alone. She needed us to literally hold her hands, and tell her we loved her." Tabitha had thought too much about this following Beth's death and funeral, and Carrie was the only one in her world she could confide in. Because she was there. And because she loved Beth equally as much.

"So what?" Carrie was bitter. *"She should have cried out for our help before she forced that blade into her chest."* Carrie had already reached the stage of grief where anger had surfaced.

"It's okay to be mad at her, you know," Tabitha had told her then. *"But the important thing to remember is she left this world loving us. She may have felt like she had no way out, but she knew we loved her and that we tried everything to help her. She just couldn't do it anymore."*

"Why do you do that? Better yet, how? How can you keep such a level head? I am moving from moment to moment, barely holding myself up." Carrie raised her voice and then turned away. *"I can't even look at you!"*

"Well you're going to have to," Tabitha spoke calmly and sounded more reserved than she felt when she initially walked through the gallery and stood at the doorway of Carrie's studio. *"I'm not leaving here until we work through this anger and confusion. And for what it's worth, I cannot sleep, I barely eat, and I am not fucking fine."*

Carrie turned to look at the one dearest friend she had left, but she said nothing in response to her honest and true words. She did have a sudden sense of relief knowing that she was not alone in feeling weak and helpless. Beth's death was still incredibly raw and painful, and up until that moment, she felt as if Tabitha had been better at handling their loss, just as she believed Tabitha was always better at everything.

"I want to talk to you about the last time you had contact with Beth before that night," Tabitha began, and Carrie shook her head in refusal. *"Why not? Are you keeping something from me? Did you two argue? It doesn't matter if you did, you know. None of that mattered in the end."*

Carrie backed up from being in such close proximity to Tabitha. She was already crying. *"We were here,"* Carrie referred to being in the studio. *"Beth came by, and she was the worst I've ever seen her. She was spiraling. And I'd had it with being loving and supportive of her craziness. Yes, I know she loved Joe Morgan. But it all became an unhealthy obsession for her. I know she was hurting. I was just so sick and tired of encouraging her to hang in there, and suggesting she maybe give it time, and so on. I was done with telling her what she wanted to hear. I came unglued. I told her she needed to get on with her life. Her life. Not some fairytale life she imagined living with Joe Morgan. I told her she was not acting like the Bethie that I knew and loved. And that she needed to get herself together and regain her courage and self respect."* Tabitha's expression did not change as she listened. Carrie was never blunt in a hurtful way with anyone. Tabitha, however, had made numerous efforts with Beth to show her tough, but genuine love, and tell her like it was. *"She asked me if that's how I really saw her. She was so taken aback by my words. I was downright mean and hurtful, and I hate myself so much for that now. What if I pushed her to the breaking point? What if I was the one she needed to pull her from the edge — and I failed her?"*

"You don't think I feel the same way? Get off your pious pedestal, Carrie! We were both her best friends. The three of us had something so damn special, so rare. But neither one of us could save her. It doesn't matter what you said, or I said, or what either of us didn't say. Beth couldn't handle herself anymore. She was so far gone. She wasn't in a healthy frame of mind. No amount of medication or love from the two of us could save her. Please realize that, because I know I cannot take losing you. Be angry! Be sad! Grieve for fuck's sake! But please, do not do it without me." Carrie saw the tears on Tabitha's face, and she in turn reached for her with open arms. They held onto each other with the strength they had left, and

their sobs echoed in that room. *"I've blamed myself, too."* Carrie heard Tabitha admit in barely a whisper as she pulled out of their close embrace. *"Medically, I failed when I couldn't do anything to help her, to keep her here with us."*

Carrie used her thumbs to gently wipe away the tears from Tabitha's cheeks. *"We are both doing it. Blaming ourselves for Beth's choice, when it was something so out of our control. That's easy to say, I know, and it's also impossible to completely grasp."*

"She would absolutely hate to see what this is doing to us," Tabitha stated, as a matter of fact.

"I know that," Carrie agreed.

"Then promise me, from here on, we stop. We have to keep each other up. No more pointing fingers or shutting the other one out. I swear to you, I'll beat the shit out of you if you stop loving me or stop wanting me in your life." Tabitha tried to crack a smile as she spoke, but instead she broke into another sob.

Carrie grabbed her by the shoulders, hard, and forced to her to look at her. *"Tab. You have always unnerved me. You're the most beautiful bitch in my world. I need you, probably much more than you need or want me, so you're stuck. I'm going to love on you forever."* The two of them managed to giggle through their runny noses and tears. All they had left was each other. Sure, they had their husbands and children, but it wasn't the same as the trio that formed the solid bond of forever friendship in college. And now there were just two. *A duo.*

Carrie stood in wet paint droplets on the bare, stripped floorboard of her studio. She blinked away a few tears as she brought herself back to reality. She needed to paint something. Something substantial. And she was going to do it today.

Chapter Five

After lack of sleep, fighting a hangover headache, and having an emotionally draining day, Tabitha made her way home from the hospital. She kicked off her clogs at the door. She sterilized them at the hospital so any traces of the day, in an often-times messy emergency room, were now gone. She walked in socks toward the kitchen, where the aroma of something cooking told her that was where she would find her husband.

"Hey Tab," Rory greeted her, turning his body halfway around from the stovetop to give her a peck on the lips.

"You taste like marinara sauce. Is it a spaghetti night?" Rory was a better cook than she, and Tabitha was starving for anything tonight. His Italian dishes were her favorite though. "Nope," he replied. "Chicken parmesan over pasta."

"Mmm," she nodded, as she swung open the refrigerator in search of a bottle of wine. She bent down and peered her head further inside.

"I think we're out," he stated as a matter of fact, knowing what she wanted. Rory rarely drank alcohol and it secretly unnerved him when Tabitha thought she had to drink wine like most people put down water.

"What? There isn't any in the fridge in the garage either? Shit. You could have picked up a bottle if you were at the store for these ingredients," Tabitha gestured her hand toward the stovetop.

Rory shrugged. And Tabitha tried not to react to that. "How long until dinner?" She assumed the boys were home, in their rooms doing homework or downstairs in the basement playing video games.

"Ten minutes," he smiled halfheartedly, and held his breath as he knew what she was calculating in her mind.

"Be right back," she said, in a rush to leave the kitchen to retrieve her shoes and keys by the front door.

"Seriously Tab? You just got here!"

"Wine run. I'll be quick. Promise!"

31

During dinner, the boys kept the conversation lively. There never was a dull moment raising boys, and Tabitha thrived at being a boy mom. She knew how to interfere to play referee when they threw their fists, and she was especially good at acting unfazed with their inappropriate nature. *What was it with boys and their fascination with butts and farting anyway?* Dillon, twelve years old, was *pumped*, as he described it, to go to the middle school basketball game the following evening. He didn't play basketball, but he was a pretty good first baseman for the middle school's baseball team. Tabitha watched him speak. He had always looked like his father, but in his preteen years he was beginning to favor him so much more. Thick brown hair, and those bushy eyebrows over striking hazel eyes. The way he moved his mouth when he spoke, and of all his expressions were Rory through and through. His forehead was breaking out in tiny pink pimples, and Tabitha thought to remind him again to use the dermatologist-prescribed facial cream twice a day after he showered, morning and night.

"Are you going dad?" Dillon broke her thought when he spoke to Rory.

"Heck yeah, I wouldn't miss it!" It was a regional championship game, and Hays Middle School had not had a basketball team advance that far in the playoffs for more than a decade.

"Can I too, dad?" their youngest, Dane, spoke up.

"Absolutely," Rory told him, as he looked at Tabitha, having read her mind. "It starts at six, babe." Tabitha had her third consecutive twelve-hour shift to work tomorrow that ended at six in the evening.

"I guess I'm on my own for dinner then, as I know the three of you will be eating popcorn and nachos in the gymnasium." Her youngest giggled.

"Every chef gets a night off," Rory stated, taking the last bite of the chicken parmesan on his plate.

"Of course," Tabitha smiled. "And this was delicious by the way." She used her fork to point down at her plate of food, which she had eaten at least half. She finished off the wine in the glass in front of her when Dane watched her closely.

"I thought mom didn't have any more wine!" Dane declared just as a nine year old would, and Tabitha saw how Rory shot him a look. *Disapproval? Shut the hell up!* She could effortlessly read all of her boys, her husband included.

"I just bought this tonight, before dinner," she creased her brow at Rory and then looked back at Dane. Dillon was too focused on eating again to notice, or care what they were speaking of now. If it didn't pertain to sports, he tuned out.

"Dad poured out the bottle you had left in the refrigerator." Her youngest son had a sweet, round, innocent face with features that Tabitha couldn't deny were her own. His hair was light and his eyes were brown. He had a patch of freckles across the bridge of his nose, as Tabitha also had and used makeup to conceal.

"He did?" Tabitha looked at her husband to question him, as he tipped back the iced water in his glass.

"It was stale, bud. I told you that." Rory only made eye contact with their little boy.

"Day old wine, with a twist cap, is not stale. That was mine from last night. Seriously Rory? I could have saved myself a trip back out tonight to the store." Tabitha watched him stand up from the table, preparing to clear his plate and Dane's.

"Or you could have drank water like the rest of us."

That was all that was said. The boys were suddenly more interested in their cell phones and making their way out of the kitchen before they were told to help load the dishwasher or take out the trash. Or witness an argument between their parents.

Tabitha watched Rory busy himself near the trash can, which he had pulled out of the pantry. He scraped the plates clean, and then flipped down the door of the dishwater as he prepared to load it. This wasn't at all unusual for him. Rory took care of most of what needed to be done inside of their house. Out of spite, and because she really did want more, Tabitha poured herself another glass of chardonnay on the counter, right beside Rory.

"Since when does my having a glass of wine with dinner bother you?" She watched him look up from bending over near the dishwasher.

"That's not just a glass. You've poured your second. And how many more will you suck down before bedtime?"

"Rory, I work twelve-hour days. If I need a glass of wine to unwind, or smooth the edges off, I'm going to have it." Tabitha stood against the counter with her lower back against it. She had changed into a pair of black yoga pants and a sleeveless black v-neck t-shirt. Her arms were folded across her chest, her pedicured-feet were bare and her toenails were polished fire red. Her hair was tied back into a high ponytail, and when she spoke it bobbed atop her head. Tabitha was the sexiest woman in the world to Rory. When he won her heart a dozen years ago, he swore he would do anything to keep her happy. *She was his.* But since that night she watched her best friend die, she had not been the same. Her desire for a glass a wine *to take the edges off the day* had become a need. A real, undeniable need. He was worried about his wife.

Rory uprighted himself from the dishwasher. In socks, he stood, at most, two inches taller than his wife. He wore faded denim and a tight black t-shirt. They made a striking couple, who produced two handsome sons. He stepped closer to her. She took one more sip of the wine in the glass she held, and intentionally kept holding it as he moved toward her.

"I know you work really hard, and long hours," he began. "I try to take care of everything around here so you do not have to do too much when you get home, when you're tired and worn out. I know you've always been the girl who needs something to unwind." He didn't want to add *with alcohol,* but he most definitely had thought it. "I'm just seeing you drink more lately, since Beth died. I want you to talk to me if you're hurting. You don't have to have another drink to suppress your feelings. I'm here. I can listen. I will hold you when you need me to."

Tabitha willed away the tears in her eyes that were fighting to fill up and spill over. She nodded, and then made the conscious effort to set down her glass on the counter behind her. She reached for him. She wrapped her arms around his neck, as he pulled her close by her waist. And then he heard her say, softly, in his ear, "I'm trying." And she meant those words. She was giving it her best effort to handle what haunted her. But it felt like a losing battle almost all of the time. Alcohol was the only thing she had found to numb the pain for a little while.

Chapter Six

Twenty four hours later, Carrie stood on the bare, stripped floorboards in her studio. The gallery was dark, and closed for the night. She had just dropped off the twins for the highly anticipated regional basketball game at the middle school. Their volleyball practice had been canceled for the evening, so they were wound up and giddy when Carrie dropped them off. Sheridan was the more reserved and responsible child of the twins, while Jess was reckless and incorrigible sometimes. Carrie counted on one eleven year old to keep an eye on the other — all of the time.

She stared at the painting in front of her. It was coming along. There were vibrant, attractive colors to this one. Finally. She was coming out of her dark slump. The text tone from her phone forced her out of her creative thought. She had a wet paint brush in hand, and set it down on the easel's ledge to retrieve her phone on the table across the room. She couldn't ignore it, just in case it was one of her girls.

I'm parked out front. Can I come in and interrupt the artist at work? It was Tabitha.

Carrie smiled. She could only count on one hand the times that Tabitha had stopped by her studio, impromptu, in recent years. That was something Beth always did. But since they lost Beth, Tabitha had assumed that role. They never spoke of it though.

You're never an interruption. Meet me at the door.

The lights were dim in the gallery as Carrie turned the lock and pulled open the door to find Tabitha, in her typical navy blue scrubs and matching rubber clogs, standing on the front step.

"Hey," Carrie greeted her first with open arms and Tabitha gave her a tight hug. "Headed home from the hospital?"

"Yes, but no one is home tonight. Rory and the boys are at the game. He texted me and said your girls were there, so I took a chance to see if you'd be here."

"Always," Carrie smiled. The olive green bibbed overalls she wore had dried paint stains spattered across the front. "Come on back."

Tabitha followed Carrie through the gallery with no lights on. The studio was the complete opposite, lit up and bright when they entered it. Tabitha's eyes always went to the paint-splattered bare hardwood flooring first. It undoubtedly added character to the studio like nothing else. There was a cherry red sofa against the far wall, and a tall table with two high-back chairs, and a small refrigerator in the corner. Otherwise, there were things only an artist knew what to do with that were set up and displayed all over the room. The easel with the painting on it, in the center of the cluttered but organized space, caught Tabitha's eye. She, however, dismissed it for a moment when Carrie spoke.

"Wanna sit? I know after twelve hours you're tired and hungry. If I kept a schedule like you, I would fall into bed the moment I got home."

"You would not. You're anal about dinner on the table and bellies full," Tabitha teased her, as she made the effort to tuck one of the defiant blonde curls behind her best girlfriend's ear for her, and then she stepped past her to take a closer look at the unfinished painting.

Carrie laughed, and agreed. "Guilty." Then she followed Tabitha to the easel she had been standing in front of for two days. She was curious of her opinion.

"The leaves, low on those trees…and the busy, bustling street with the buildings so close together. An umbrella table, that bright yellow umbrella. A table for three? You're painting Europe, aren't you?" Tabitha spoke about everything she saw.

Carrie nodded. "It's already titled, 'The trip not taken.' The umbrella had to be yellow, just like the one on our patio at the apartment, remember?"

"Old and tattered but we really thought we found a gem at that yard sale off campus." Tabitha giggled. Even though Carrie was wealthy now, she still appreciated the great finds, or the old, refurbished treasures.

"It was a gem!" Carrie defended the purchase she made back then.

"I wish we could have taken that trip." The three of them going to Europe, someday, had been on their never-ending bucket list. "This is going to be beautiful when you're finished painting it. And if I had thousands of dollars lying around, I would be your first buyer."

Carrie wanted to say she could have it if she wanted it, if she still loved it when it was completed. Instead, she focused on Tabitha's insinuation that money was tight in her home. "Rory hasn't had any luck finding a job yet?" Carrie lost track of how long it had been since Tabitha's husband lost his job as a project manager of a construction company in Hays that had filed for bankruptcy.

"He's had two interviews in the last two years. He doesn't even mention looking for a job anymore. He's enjoying being Mr. Mom." Tabitha rolled her eyes.

"That works for you guys though, right?" Tabitha's senior nursing position at the hospital carried them financially, or so Carrie had thought.

"It works from paycheck to paycheck. There's just not a lot of saving for the future going on in our house." Tabitha refrained from mentioning how she oftentimes spends money they do not have — for things like manicures, pedicures, her gym membership and personal trainer. And wine. She refused to make sacrifices.

Carrie watched Tabitha walk across the room, over to the refrigerator in the corner. "Bottled water or diet coke," Carrie called out. It wasn't very well stocked with much else.

"How about that bottle of wine stashed in the back?" Tabitha grinned and reached for it without permission.

"Help yourself, but all I have are paper cups."

"Straight from the bottle never bothered me either," Tabitha laughed at her own comment. "Want some?"

"None for me. I am trying a new fad diet this week, and I've already exceeded my calorie limit today," Carrie admitted, but looked discouraged.

"Go liquid only, and the pounds will fall off." Tabitha glanced over at her and raised the bottle before she poured the Foris Moscato for herself in a paper cup.

"Is that your secret?" Carrie asked, feeling as if she was calling her out on something. And the look on Tabitha's face when she turned around told her she comprehended it that way as well.

"Have you been talking to Rory?" Tabitha asked, as she walked toward the sofa that Carrie had already plopped down on.

"No. Why?"

"He threw out my wine at home, and I drove off right before dinner to pick up more."

"Because you had to have it?" Carrie wondered if Tabitha's habit to drink a glass now and then, or daily, had become something more. This was the first time she had raided the mini refrigerator in the studio on her way home from work. Not that Carrie minded. She had just taken note.

"Yeah," Tabitha answered without questioning herself, or Carrie for asking. "I do have to have it. Does that make me a falling down drunk? No."

"Did Rory accuse you of something?"

"Not really, no. He's worried about me, he said, because my alcohol intake has increased since we lost Beth."

Carrie was close enough to Tabitha to reach her, and without a second thought, she took the plastic cup from her hands and brought it to her own mouth for a generous sip. So much for counting calories for her diet. Tabitha's eyes widened before she laughed out loud. "I will not fault you if you need to chase away the pain. I probably should turn to alcohol instead of food," Carrie attempted a smile, as she handed back the cup. The mention of their great loss instantly pained her.

"I knew you would get it."

"That's why you're here? For me to tell you that drinking wine in excess is okay because we are grieving?"

"No," Tabitha responded. "I just can't talk to anyone else about it. Rory is a part of the world that has gone on."

"He wants to help you though. You said so yourself, he's concerned. Tab, take it from me, if your husband reaches out to you to talk, or to get naked — reach back."

"Oh honey," Tabitha said, as she squeezed Carrie's knee. "Enough about my potential drinking problem and jobless husband. How are things with Dom and the girls?"

Carrie again reached for the paper cup from Tabitha. She took another swig from it, and then got up from the sofa to refill it with the bottle of wine that Tabitha had left sitting out on the table. *She knew she would want more.*

"He works too much," Carrie said as she sat back down and handed the refill back to Tabitha. "He makes a shitload of money for our family. The girls adore him, and he's very good at making up for lost time —with them— when he's around."

"What about with you?"

"We haven't had sex since before Beth died."

Tabitha's eyes widened. "That's been seven months. Carrie…"

Carrie could hear the accusation in Tabitha's voice. "Don't say it. He's not cheating on me. He's just a workaholic. But, I do wonder if we will ever be close again. Not just sex. I miss talking to him about nothing at all, instead of just feeling detached while discussing the front and center things in our lives regarding the girls or the next big purchase we will make."

"Tell him that, Care."

"There's never a good time when you know your husband isn't really listening."

"Damn. Listen to us," Tabitha said. "I'm bitching about home-cooked meals minus the wine, and you need to get laid and have a genuine conversation afterward. Or vice versa."

"Instead, we're here, on this old couch — that I seriously picked up at a thrift store two decades ago — and we're sharing a paper cup of wine," Carrie laughed as she spoke.

"It's really good though," Tabitha lifted the cup to her mouth again.

"Save some more for me," Carrie bossed her, and then Tabitha handed her the rest of the wine that was left in their shared paper cup.

Chapter Seven

Tabitha left the studio when the basketball game ended. She had known it was over when Carrie received a text from the twins that they were ready to be picked up. Carrie mentioned following Tabitha out, but she ended up staying behind a few additional minutes to seal the paints, turn off the lights, and lock up. She stepped off the curb near her vehicle on the street, lit with a pole light above her. She clicked the unlock button and started the engine from the key remote in her hand. As she reached for her door handle, she heard someone behind her. Startled, Carrie turned around quickly. The wind was blowing crazily again and her hair blew in her face.

"Nice night, huh?"

Carrie pushed her hair away from her eyes and froze at the sight of him. In broad daylight, Joe Morgan freaked her out. *What the hell was he doing near her in the dark of night, outside of her studio, waiting for her?* Strangely, he was wearing all dark clothing, just as she specifically imagined he would be in that painting with Beth.

"What are you doing out here?" she asked, as she consciously swung opened the door to her SUV. Her cell phone was in her hand and she was not going to hesitate to dial for emergency help.

"Out walking," he told her.

"Well keep walking," she spat back at him, and moved her body into the driver's seat.

"Beth wouldn't approve of how you girls react to me."

"Do not speak her name to me. You have no right!" Carrie could feel her heart pounding in her chest, and she could hear the pulse of it in her own ears. *Like hell Beth wouldn't approve!* She again stared, or more like glared, at his dark eyes, dark hair, dark clothing. He wasn't shady, but he was disturbing. He had only brought trouble to Beth's life.

"She wanted for us to get along."

"You're one to talk about knowing what she wanted." Carrie spoke through clenched teeth. She was eager to slam the door to her vehicle and shut him out.

"That's harsh, but true," he replied, and Carrie finally closed the space between them with an abruptly slammed and locked car door. She forced the gear shift into drive and immediately pressed her foot down hard on the gas pedal. Joe Morgan had to take a hurried step backward to avoid being in the way. Carrie never looked back. Not even a glance into her rearview mirror. Both of her hands on the steering wheel in front of her were trembling. *What could Joe Morgan possibly want with her?*

Carrie had tried to call Tabitha while she drove, but her attempt to reach her went to voicemail. She most likely was already at home and distracted, so Carrie never left her a message. She just drove straight to pick up the twins. And then all she wanted was to go home. She hoped Dom would be there by now. Her strange encounter with Joe Morgan had shaken her up.

The girls were bickering on the way home about a boy on the basketball team, and Carrie found herself zoning in and out of their argument. As soon as they pulled into the garage at home, Carrie spoke. "Showers and homework girls!"

Sheridan, the more compassionate of the twins, was sitting in the passenger seat, and she turned her head to look at her mother. "Is something wrong, mom?" she asked, before she not so subtly shifted her body in the direction of the backseat to make quick eye contact with her sister. "You've been kind of quiet, and now we're suddenly getting barked at." They both had mentioned to their mother before the game that their homework was already done. She had obviously forgotten.

"I'm fine. Just tired. And I'm telling you both that it's late and you need to take showers and get ready for bed."

"Homework's done!" Jess spoke up from the backseat as if she was guaranteeing permission to stay up late watching Friends on Netflix, which was what Carrie was well aware she did most school nights. She was seriously considering giving that child coffee in the morning to counteract her awful mood. She was a night owl and an incorrigible morning person.

"Upstairs, girls," Carrie told them again.

They were fighting over who was going to shower first when Tabitha passed their bedrooms and both of their doors were wide open. She stayed out of it, because she was en route to her own room, where she expected to find Dom. His car was parked in the garage, but he wasn't anywhere on the main floor of the house. That house was just too massive to call out to anyone.

When she walked through the open doorway of their bedroom, he was in there, sitting on the ivory-colored sofa that was a part of the mini living area in that immense space for a bedroom. He had his cell phone pressed to his ear, which was no surprise to her. He made eye contact with her and she waved. Dom was still wearing his black suit pants, white dress shirt, sans a tie now. His belly folded over his belt. His face was full, and his chin doubled. The short-cropped haircut, that he had opted for when his hair began to thin, appeared grayer to her tonight. Father Time had touched him, too.

Any other night, she would have gone in the shower and left him be. Tonight, she wanted his attention as soon as he ended his phone call. He saw her staring. Waiting for him, obviously. He wrapped up the phone call quickly. *Had he done that for her?* And then she spoke first.

"Hi. All done for the night?"

"Hi hon. I think so, yes. I'm beat. Mind if I step in front of you for the shower?" Carrie thought of her girls, fighting over who was going to go in their bathroom and shower first. And then she remembered Tabitha's words. *You need to get laid and have a genuine conversation afterward.*

"Go ahead," she began, "or we could both go in together…"

The look on Dom's face was sheer surprise. He chuckled a little, as if she was kidding and he was supposed to react to the joke. Carrie never laughed. Especially when he walked past her and closed the bathroom door behind him.

She sunk down onto those ivory sofa cushions, feeling defeated. She hadn't told him about the scare she had felt being approached by Joe Morgan outside of her gallery. They just didn't know how to talk to each other anymore. And making love was obviously out of the question.

Her phone buzzed in her pocket.

I missed a call from you! Can it wait until tomorrow? I'm headed to bed.

There was no need to keep Tabitha awake. It wasn't urgent. It was over.

Not important. Night night.

The following morning, Tabitha had the day off. After having put in thirty-six hours in three days at the hospital, she needed a breather. She heard Rory's alarm sound on his side of their bed. She peeled her eyes. "Why do the nights always go so fast?" she whined.

"Go back to sleep," he told her. "I'm going to make pancakes for the boys before school. I'll bring you one in bed…"

She attempted a tired laugh. "That might be too sticky for the sheets."

"Talking dirty already? Gonna be a good day off." Rory chuckled as he got out of their bed. She watched him slip on a pair of plaid lounge pants and pull a t-shirt over his head. And then she closed her eyes again.

Twenty minutes later, Tabitha was merely lying there with her eyes closed, but she had not been able to fall back to sleep. Her body was programmed to wake up early and get moving. And besides, she could hear the boys getting ready, and she wanted to see them off. They were growing entirely too fast, at twelve and nine years old. She should be soaking up all of her time with them. Tabitha threw back the covers and planted her bare feet, fire red polished toes, on the carpet.

She brushed her teeth and washed her face with cold water. She pulled up her hair and knotted it on top of her head, before she slipped on her white terrycloth robe overtop of the narrow-strapped, low-support sports bra and boyshorts she had worn to bed.

In the kitchen, she stood in the doorway watching Rory. His pants hung low on his waist and his t-shirt was snug fitting around his biceps and torso. He was talking nonstop as he flipped more pancakes on the griddle. The boys were already digging their forks into the stack of pancakes on their plates.

"Seriously guys, you'll find no better pancakes in all of Hays. You know your mom can't make a flapjack to save her life..."

"Hey!" Tabitha came through the doorway, clearly offended, and her littlest boy giggled. She squeezed both of her sons from behind as they sat side by side on stools, eating their breakfast at the island.

Rory laughed out loud when he saw her and heard her protest. "Can I get you one, Tab?"

"A very small one, and I'll drizzle the syrup on it — you're way too generous and my thighs can't handle it." She was headed to the gym this morning and feeling overly stuffed full of flour and sugar was not a part of her plan.

The four of them ate breakfast together before the boys reacted to the horn that honked from out on the driveway. It was the neighbor lady's turn to drive the carpool to school today, which explained why Rory was still in his pajama pants in the kitchen. Tabitha watched her boys grab their backpacks and cell phones. She snuck a kiss on top of Dane's head and Dillon mumbled his goodbye, sans eye contact, before he let the door slam behind him.

"Those two," Rory bobbed his head and grinned. "The light of my life."

Tabitha stared at him for a moment.

"What?" he asked her, drinking the last of the milk in his tall glass and leaving a visible mustache on his top lip.

"You're such a good daddy," she praised him. And sincerely meant her words.

"I want to be here for them. Always. I think losing my job a couple years ago was the best thing that could have happened. We are closer, the guys and me, because I'm able to be here." Tabitha took a deep breath, slowly, through her nostrils. But that also meant she had to work her ass off to make ends meet. Sixty hour work weeks were beginning to do her in at forty years old. *And forty was hardly old!*

"Rory, all dads who work are still able to successfully parent, provide for, and love their children."

"Oh I know that. This just works so well for us."

"We never agreed that not having a second income was going to be good for us. I was never okay with that." Tabitha pushed her plate forward. She had eaten half the scrumptious pancake. She sipped her orange juice now, which she had poured in a stemless wine glass, and awaited her husband's response. She felt like this conversation was long overdue for the two of them.

"I know. Of course I am aware of that," Rory began, "and if something comes up, I'll jump on it."

"But you're no longer looking?" It had been two years, and Tabitha assumed that much about him a long while ago. Waiting for something to fall into his lap was not happening. Or maybe, he wasn't waiting at all?

"I don't know what I want to do anymore. Getting back into construction now, with guys twice as young as me, just feels degrading."

Tabitha was beginning to fully understand this. Rory had genuine fears about returning to the working world. Still, she needed him to find a job again. *Suck it up. Deal.* "I hear what you're saying, I do. I just need for you to realize that we have college in our future for two boys, and I don't want to have to keep my grueling schedule at the hospital for the next twenty years."

Rory nodded his head in silence, and she watched him wipe off the milk from his upper lip with the back of his hand. God, she loved him. Looking at him, sitting there with rumpled hair, and a scruffy face. His hazel eyes drew her in every time he looked at her. And this time was no different.

"I'm not harping or bitching at you. I completely understand how you must be feeling. You do so much for me and the boys, and around this house. I don't take any of that, or you, for granted."

"You just need me to get off my ass and get a job."

"No. That's not it at all. You are always off your ass," she laughed, "if that makes sense. You are a workhorse. We just need you to get paid for that, and soon." Rory nodded, and Tabitha spoke again. "You know I've been with Carrie a lot lately. We talk about everything. I feel for her. She's filthy rich because Dom does nothing but work. They have all they could possibly want for themselves and their family, but..."

"But what?" He wanted to know what they didn't have, because he too felt envious of all of their money, their mansion on the hill, and top-of-the-line material things.

"They seem to have lost each other along the way. That huge house needs more love and memories, like a home should have. Like ours."

"Dom seems really good with the girls, and they appear to adore him," Rory noted.

"He is, and they do," Tabitha agreed. "It's Carrie. They're not close anymore. I'm not sure what kind of marriage can exist without communication — and intimacy."

"They don't talk much?" Rory inquired.

Tabitha shook her head. "And it's been several months since they've had sex."

"Damn," Rory ran his fingers through his hair. "Do you think Dom has—"

"Someone else?" Tabitha interjected. "Carrie swears not. She said she would know."

"Tab, how naïve. Men have needs."

"Uh hello?" Tabitha confronted him. "Women have the same needs for affection and attention, if not more so."

"Oh yeah?" Rory chuckled.

"Uh huh," she replied, standing up from the stool at the island that was adjacent to his. She meant to give him a quick peck on the lips, but he pulled her closer by the belt of her robe. Their kiss deepened. She could taste the syrup on his lips, his tongue, and deeper in his mouth. Her robe was now completely open and her husband's hands were on her body.

"The kitchen…we should clean up," she spoke with her mouth still on his, and he nibbled the tip of her tongue with his teeth.

"Later. I need to wish my wife a proper good morning." Rory cupped her breast as he kissed her hard and full on the mouth. He moved his hand lower, overtop her toned abs, and even lower. He slipped his entire hand inside of her lacy boyshorts and she moaned.

A moment later, she dragged him by the hand, running and tripping twice over the belt of her terrycloth robe that hung loose. They laughed out loud. They made it to their bedroom and onto the disheveled and still unmade bed. Her robe was off and underneath her, as Rory stretched his t-shirt overtop of his head and off. Tabitha reached for the elastic waistband of his pants. She stretched it just far enough for his manhood to spring up and into her hand. She didn't resist. She stroked him. He lunged forward and found her mouth again with his own. He stretched and tugged at the material of her bra and moved it away from her breasts and found her with his mouth, while his opposite hand found her core. His fingers showed her no mercy. And she wasn't about to beg for him to stop. Her bra was on the floor now and her boyshorts were at her ankles. Her body throbbed at his every touch. At the moment of her intense release, Rory was there. Moving on top of her. Entering her. Pleasing her. Pleasing himself. Sex. Making love. Wanting each other had only enhanced in their marriage. He called out her name as he buried his head into her bare chest. Tabitha ran her fingers through his messy hair, and smiled.

That was them. They knew how to get lost in each other. It was effortless. It was intoxicating. Reality would eventually come around again though. Per their earlier conversation in the kitchen, Rory needed to begin again with his job search. No more hesitation. No more excuses.

Chapter Eight

The contrast of her dark, almost black, hair and her porcelain skin tone was striking. Ever since she was a little girl, even strangers commented on her beauty. *She's going to be a heartbreaker.* As life turned out, Beth Louden most definitely had done her share of dishing out heartbreak. But being on the receiving end of it blindly forced her to believe there was no way back from the edge. Not after she had finally fallen body and soul for one particular man. And her heartbreak inevitably broke her.

He had dark hair, dark eyes, and he was at least a few inches over six feet tall. His shoulders were broad, and his build was one of a man who was no outsider to the gym. Beth could imagine his intense full-body workouts. *Or perhaps he was merely blessed with a great body.* At first glance, Beth was taken. Taken in. And taken aback.

She wanted to know who he was. *What was his name, his story, and most of all — was he attached?* She wanted his attention. For him to know her. All of her life, Beth had been a believer in love at first glance. She wasn't entirely convinced that she was *in love* with a man she didn't even know. But she was in awe of how she felt at the initial moment she saw Joe Morgan.

Beth had stopped in at Gutch's Bar and Grill on Seventh Street in Hays. Her work day had ended and she was headed home, alone. Her secretary at the downtown office, where Beth was a social worker, had been talking about the must-try brick oven pizzas at Gutch's. Tonight was as good of a night as any since Beth rarely cooked for one. She called ahead to order and had just stopped in for the carry-out. She walked in and directly up to the bar. The lights were dimmed, the noise of people talking hummed in the air. It was after five o'clock and the dinner crowd was on the verge of being in full swing. Almost every stool at the bar was already occupied.

She waited at the far end of that bar. She told the bartender that she had a carry-out order for Elizabeth. And then she saw him. There was one vacant bar stool between them. He appeared to be alone, and he was drinking whatever kind of beer was on tap. She wondered if he was having a drink while he waited for his own carry-out order. *A drink wasn't a bad idea. But Beth assumed her pizza was almost ready.*

He looked up from his beer and caught her staring. She smiled with closed-lips. It was an attempted polite smile, to offer nothing over the top that would give her emotions away. She felt jittery and excited. He spoke before she completely turned her head away.

"Elizabeth? A traditional good-girl name." He had overheard her give the bartender her name for her order. *He was listening. Looking at her. And he was interested.*

Beth grinned, even though she was undecided if she should be flattered or offended. She was hardly a good girl. But she wasn't a bad girl either. And he was ridiculously good-looking. "Traditional, yes. Good girl, well, that's debatable."

He chuckled at her response before he took a long swig from his glass. The bartender interrupted. "Elizabeth? The capacity of our brick oven is full tonight. Your pizza is second in line. It should just be about eight more minutes."

Beth nodded, "Not a problem," and she turned the end stool at the bar so she could sit down. The bartender then offered her a drink while she waited. *On the house, in appreciation for your patience.* Beth didn't think twice. She asked for a chardonnay.

There was still one empty bar stool between her and that dazzling man. Beth turned to him, and noticed he was finishing off the last of his beer.

"Are you waiting for an order?" she asked him, after she took a generous sip of her wine. It wasn't that she needed the courage to speak to a man. She had never left the dating scene. She was still in it, full throttle. She just had not had anyone serious, or long-term, in her life since her brief marriage and divorce after college.

"No," he turned to her. "Just having a beer, or two, tonight." Beth wondered if, like her, he had no one to go home to.

"I'm Beth Louden. I'm a native of Hays, and social work is how I make a living." She cursed herself for sounding like a school girl.

She watched him finger the empty glass in front of him before he spoke. She definitely wondered if she had been too forthcoming. *Had she come across as odd or weird?* And then he spoke in return. "Helping people. I could have guessed you were one of those. I'm Joe Morgan, not a native of Hays. I'm a beer distributor."

"I'll take what you said as compliment. I enjoy helping people. It's nice to meet you, Joe." Beth smiled, and she watched him completely turn his body on the stool toward her. His legs were long, thick, and muscular.

"Who's waiting for that pizza at home? I'll bet my next beer that a boring husband and two or three kids are looking for you right now." Beth caught on quickly. He was searching to find out more about her, to know if she was attached. This wasn't her first rodeo of getting to know a man. A part of her ached for exactly what he described — a husband and children of her own.

"No one, actually. All alone am I."

"You're too beautiful for that."

Something surged her insides. It was more than a fluttery, flirty feeling. Beth tipped back her wine glass, and sincerely told him, "thank you."

"Another beer Joe?" the bartender interrupted them. He was holding Beth's to-go pizza box in one hand. This was Beth's cue to stand up, take it, and leave. But she didn't do any of that.

"Yes, he'll have another beer, and I'm going to make this carry-out a dine-in." The bartender nodded as Beth placed the pizza box on the bar top in the middle of her and Joe Morgan. She flipped the lid. "What are you waiting for? Help me eat this. Going home alone, just yet, doesn't appeal to me tonight."

Joe's facial expression changed. He liked her. She knew that. She could see it, and already feel it.

The conversation at the bar during their first night together was both effortless and mysterious. And at closing time, neither one of them were ready to say goodnight. Joe Morgan walked her to her car in the well-lit parking lot. There was a gentleman side and bad-boy streak to him. Beth was attracted to both. No one else was around outside, in the windy night air, when she backed up against her car door, stood up on her tip toes, and let Joe Morgan kiss her for the first time.

She had only drank three glasses of wine. She wasn't intoxicated by the alcohol, but she was under the influence of him. Their kisses deepened. Their hands touched each other in places that meant they should undeniably be behind closed doors. And then Beth heard herself say, *follow me home.*

It was, without a doubt, the best sex Beth had ever had. His size. His attention to her body, her needs. He wasn't a selfish lover by any means. And Beth made every effort to drive him to the edge with desire. The seductive, slow, way she touched him, everywhere. How passionately she kissed him, everywhere. She watched his eyes roll back. She heard his moans. There was absolutely no possible way, in Beth's mind, that this was just going to be a one night stand. And then the following morning, she woke up alone.

She didn't have his phone number, and he didn't have hers. It disheartened her to think that he left her, and left her bed, without saying a word. This wasn't goodbye though. There may have been twenty-plus thousand people walking around Hays, but Beth was determined to see Joe Morgan again.

He soaked up her every thought the morning after — and all day long. After work, she drove straight to Carrie's studio and called Tabitha to meet them there. A request from one of them to meet up at the spur of the moment was never ignored. They made that pact the day they graduated from college and moved out of the apartment they lived in together. *No one goes through anything alone. Regardless of all-consuming busy lives and any circumstances, if it felt emergent to one, they would all unite.* There was the time that Tabitha found out she was pregnant, and she and Rory had not yet reached the serious point of talking marriage, children, or a future together. And then there was the instance when Carrie had called them together because her mother had died unexpectedly. Only one other time had Beth used their emergent pact. It was soon after she got married too young, and had serious reservations. So much so, she had contemplated and eventually took the necessary steps to have the union annulled.

Beth had their immediate attention as she stood with them on the paint-splattered floor boards. Carrie had immediately asked if she was okay. And Beth's response was, *I'm better than okay.*

She hadn't left out much detail. The bar, his striking good looks, their impromptu pizza and drinks, and the invitation for him to follow her home.

"You slept with him! Holy Christ! Do you know how long it's been since the three of us have boasted about one night stands?" Tabitha's reaction was typical. Moments, like that, sometimes brought her back to her crazier times — and she absolutely relished those flashes back to a simpler, freer, and more exciting time.

"Oh my God! You brought a complete stranger into your house, your bed? Bethie! That's risky…" Carrie was the error on the side of caution one of their trio. Some things had not changed despite time.

"Yes, I did it. We did it. And I have never felt more sure about anything in my entire life," Beth had told them then. "He's *the one*, girls. I can feel it with my entire body and soul."

"Are you sure that's not just the aftershocks of your orgasms?" Tabitha quipped, and they all three howled with laughter. Laughter that echoed in that studio until their conversation turned serious again.

"I can't believe this," Tabitha had said.

"So tell us more about him," Carrie had added. "Where's he from? What does he do for a living?"

"He lives here in Hays, and he's a beer distributor."

"Oh, for which company? Rory has a friend who drives for Donnewald. They could know each other?"

"I don't know the name of it," Beth answered, carefully. That was just one of many details for which she could not fill in the blank. Some of those questions were supposed to have been answered *the morning after* over coffee — or breakfast if he wasn't a coffee drinker. There was still so much for Beth to learn about him.

"Oh," Tabitha had shrugged.

"Okay, so we've all experienced it," Carrie began, rolling her eyes at her own admission, "but how awkward were things the next morning? Sometimes we are all a little braver in the dark."

Tabitha giggled following Carrie's comment, but Beth did not. She was preparing herself to tell them he was gone. "It was only awkward for me, I guess, when I woke up alone."

"What? He left?" Tabitha spoke up first. "Oh man, that's not good."

"Bethie…have you called him?" Carrie chimed in.

"We never shared our phone numbers."

Beth saw the look exchanged between Carrie and Tabitha. That day, that precise moment, was just the beginning of their inability to understand her relentless belief in Joe Morgan.

Chapter Nine

For two consecutive nights, Beth had gone back to Gutch's Bar and Grill. She ordered a drink and waited. At one point, she bravely asked the familiar bartender if Joe Morgan frequented that place often. The bartender remembered her. He mentioned the to-go pizza that Beth ended up sharing with Joe Morgan on the night they met. He chuckled when he spoke of it, and said that in all of his years of manning the bar, no one had ever opted to pull up a stool and share any of their food with a stranger. *That just might be one of my best impromptu pick-up tactics,* Beth had told him, and laughed at herself. It turned out that the bartender did know more than just Joe Morgan's name, and he mentioned how he actually was known to be a recurrent patron of all of the bars in Hays. Beth was up for the challenge. She knew what kind of truck he drove, considering he had followed her home in it. A black Chevy Silverado. Driving around the largest city in northwestern Kansas, in search of one of those vehicles parked at any given bar, didn't seem at all impossible to Beth. *Time consuming, and a bit obsessive, but not unattainable.* Beth did realize that Joe Morgan knew where she lived. If he wanted to see her again, he could show up at her house. Men were designed to pursue women. Waiting around for that to happen though was not Beth's style. She, after all, was the one who had made the first move on him. He stated to her more than once that he had no business being with a good girl. The good girl in Beth, however, was too far gone when she was with him. And she was going to remind him of that when she saw him again. Beth was bound and determined to make their reunion happen.

She did see him again. It was nearly three weeks later, when she had all but given up on lurking at bars and waiting to bump into him. Tabitha and Carrie both tried to steer her off of that path, and finally Beth was prepared to listen. Until she saw him driving a beer truck, in downtown Hays. She had never paid any attention to truck drivers before, but this one had a man behind the wheel who immediately caught her eye. They had been on a two-lane road, on which Beth had made a hasty U-turn and followed the beer truck into the parking lot of a convenience store. Beth was waiting for him when he climbed down from the truck.

"What are you doing? Following me?" His first words to her in weeks, since they had connected and were as intimate as a man and a woman could possibly be, were harsh. Beth chose to ignore his tone.

"Driving, like you. So you do work for Donnewald," she noted, turning her head to read the logo on the side of the truck.

He nodded. "Yes, work. Working. That's what I'm getting paid for, so I better get to it." Joe Morgan already wanted to lose her, brush her off. And Beth couldn't see that.

"Of course. I don't want to keep you from that. How about a drink later though?" There was no shame in asking him out, or making the first move. Again. Beth was on her lunch break, and headed back to the office. She had a client scheduled in less than fifteen minutes. She stood in the typical windy air, wearing a long black pencil skirt, black heels, and a white with black pinstripe long-sleeve button-down. The shirt was fitted and hugged her full breasts and thin torso. Her long dark hair hung loose, but right now in the wind she'd wished she had a hair tie. He sized her up, and she noticed. "You pick the place and meet me at six." Beth was incorrigible.

"I'm no good for you," he told her, again, in response.

"Why don't you let me decide that for myself?"

"Six o'clock. Your place."

And that was how their relationship continued. Beth pushed, Joe Morgan caved. But when he gave in, he wanted everything to be on his terms. Beth was so infatuated by him that it didn't matter to her.

He wanted sex. She did too.

She wanted communication. He would only bend so much.

And when Beth eventually wanted a commitment, Joe Morgan was done.

The two of them had spent an entire year playing a risky game with each other. Her version was delusional and make-believe. His was heartless. Beth noted them as a couple, eventually moving toward commitment and a future together. Both Tabitha and Carrie had warned her — he wasn't that kind of man. He wasn't the man for her. More than once, Beth had spotted him in public, giving his full attention to other women. That hadn't kept her from pursuing him. What finally stopped her was the final night she showed up at his house in Hays. She let herself inside, because he never locked his doors. She made her way back to his bedroom, and then she heard the shower water running in the master bathroom. She considered disrobing to join him. That's the way they connected best. She believed their passion was going to save them. It never occurred to her that, for Joe Morgan, it was just sex. Beth slowly pushed open the door and when she pulled back the shower curtain, the water was flowing downward and off of Joe's naked, flawless body. Joe cursed. *What the hell are you doing!*

Beth only stood there for a moment. *Was he ever happy to see her?* Of course she had startled him now, but he didn't recover. He stayed angry and annoyed. The water was splashing everywhere, even bouncing out of the shower base and onto the tiled floor at Beth's shoes.

Beth watched him hastily turn off the water and grab for a towel. He dabbed his face dry and then wrapped the long, white towel at his naked waist.

"I didn't mean to startle you," she offered a sincere apology.

"What will it take, Elizabeth?" Joe snapped at her, his dark locks were dripping more water onto his face and down his neck. "I've told you it's over. I don't want you. Tonight, it will be Melodi. Tomorrow, I'll want Samantha. And who knows who the day after that? I am not the man you need. I don't want to settle down and be anyone's husband, or a father to a bunch of babies. You can't change me. And I'm sick of putting up with watching you try. Get out of my life." There were harsh words from him before, but in no way as hurtful to this extreme. Or maybe, Beth just had not truly heard him until then. She felt like the one who was naked —and vulnerable— at that moment. He also had never admitted his indiscretions, and thrown them into her face like that. He had just claimed to not be a one-woman-man. And Beth honestly believed she could have changed that about him.

Beth had tears welling up in her eyes. She never before let his words sink deep. She hadn't allowed that. Because she loved him. She wanted him. No matter how warped she recognized herself as being throughout her desperate pursuit of him, she never gave up. "Go!" he yelled at her, but Beth never moved. "What is wrong with you? You're useless to me! Useless! I've done everything but put a knife through your heart to get rid of you. To break you of me!"

And finally, she darted out of there. In tears. In panic. In heartbreak. She was at a loss for how she was feeling. She never took a last look back at him. But she had heard his every word to her.

I've done everything but put a knife through your heart to get rid of you. To break you of me!

Chapter Ten

Carrie was sitting at the kitchen table, drinking her first cup of coffee. She was showered, dressed, and had already applied her makeup and blow dried her hair. She let the big, loose curls fall wherever once again. Wild blonde curls were Carrie Tyler's life-long trademark. Most days she liked her curly hair just as much as she disliked it.

The twins walked into the kitchen at the same time. It made Carrie smile to see them still do things together and as part of a routine. In the morning before school, one never came downstairs for breakfast without the other. Carrie gave endless credit to Sheridan for tolerating her sister's lack of good mood every single morning.

"Good morning, my girls," Carrie smiled at them. She got a pleasant response from Sheridan, but not from Jess. Sheridan, with a French braid in her blonde hair, was wearing black leggings and a Hays Middle School hoodie, which was yellow and black with the Falcon logo. She wore bone-colored boat shoes, barefoot. She looked trendy. She looked eleven years old. And then Carrie seized up her other daughter. Jess was wearing destroyed denim. The legs were ripped and full of numerous holes, in the knees, above them, and below them. She wore a pair of dark brown hiking boots with the laces left untied. It was her style, and Carrie often willed herself to stay silent, and not to judge or criticize. *This was just a phase. Showing too much disapproval could only make it worse, and cause her to rebel more.* But then Carrie looked at her daughter's choice for the top half of her body. It was a paper thin heather gray sweater that hung off of one shoulder. And the neck-line wasn't just in the shape of a V, it was a plunging V. She saw the black bra that her daughter was wearing. It was a padded push-up. She had only just recently budded. Her breasts were far from formed yet. The shirt was ridiculously revealing, and simply too much for an eleven year old to wear to school.

Carrie caught Sheridan looking at her a few times. She was waiting for her mother to object to her sister's wardrobe choice. She already forewarned Jess upstairs. *That shirt is not going to fly with mom.* Both of the girls grabbed bowls and a box of cereal from the cabinet, and when Jess came to the table with a gallon of milk, Carrie spoke.

"I think that sweater is a bit much for school, Jess." Carrie held her breath.

"And I think you know better than to talk to me this early in the morning."

Carrie saw Sheridan's eyes widen. She inhaled a deep, slow breath before she came unglued anyway. "We tolerate your bitchy mood every single day. You will change your shirt before we leave this house. If you do not listen to me and put on something decent, I will sit here with you while you call the middle school office to tell them you will be absent today — and why."

Jess, boldly and openly, rolled her eyes. "Where's dad?"

This unnerved Carrie more than she wanted to admit. Dom could do no wrong. Both of her girls believed as much. He wasn't present often enough to be the disciplinarian in their house. He was fun. He was their daddy. And he always said *yes*. "He's upstairs getting dressed for work." She wanted to add, *I stand by my order to force you to change your clothes before school. Don't even bother to ask him.* And then, as if on cue, Dom walked through the doorway of their kitchen. He was wearing a black suit, white shirt, red tie. His shoes caught her eye. They weren't his typical polished, flat soled, tie shoes. These were loafers. Slip-ins that Carrie had never seen before. For as long as they had been married, Dom never shopped for his own clothing. That was Carrie's area of expertise.

"My goodness, a sight to brighten the start of the day — all of my beautiful girls." Dom winked. Sheridan grinned and giggled, and wished him a good morning. Carrie was thinking how she couldn't recall the last time he had complimented her as beautiful. Jess' face lit up, and both Sheridan and Carrie watched her hurry to stand up from the table. "Daddy, you shoes look really classy. You're stylin'. And look, I'm wearing the shirt you bought me the same day that I helped you decide on which loafers to buy at the mall." Carrie had no idea when he had taken their daughter to the mall. She had an art convention that she attended the weekend before in Hays. It was a twelve-hour day for her. She assumed maybe Dom had spent some time with Jess then. Sheridan babysat on most weekends. It wasn't that she needed to earn the spending money, because Dom gave both of their girls a generous allowance. Sheridan just genuinely loved children and enjoyed mothering them. Carrie awaited Dom's reaction to the sweater and the inappropriate way that it fit their daughter. "Oh yeah, it looks great, baby doll." Carrie watched Jess lean into her father and he wrapped his arms around her and kissed the top of her head.

"Geez Jess, this is the most chatty you've ever been in the morning!" Sheridan quipped, and Jess walked by her and pulled her blonde braid. Sheridan had her mother's defiant curls, but she fought to tame them each day with a flat iron when she wasn't sporting a ponytail or braid. Jess had her father's once dark brown hair, before most of his already turned gray. Her hair had some waviness to it, and she left it that way because she liked it down to her shoulders and untamed. Her hair coincidently defined her character. The girls were fraternal twins. Sheridan looked like Carrie, and Jess favored Dom. Sheridan had a thicker build than Jess, but Jess was beginning to develop curves on her once lean frame and she relished the changes. The way she now chose showier clothing had definitely caught her mother's attention.

"Dom? Really? Her shirt is not something *we* should be allowing her to wear to middle school." Carrie had stressed the *we* in her statement, but she wasn't certain if Dom noticed.

"Oh. Then listen to your mother," Dom shrugged and looked at Jess. The shrug, from Carrie's viewpoint, was his way of taking Jess' side. *Well I think you look fine, but your mother says not...*

"No, please! You bought this for me and I want to wear it." Carrie prevented herself from rolling her eyes. *What hadn't that man bought for his girls? One shirt was hardly an unforgettable, special gift when they were both beyond spoiled.*

"We are leaving in fifteen minutes. Change or miss the entire day of school and spend all evening doing make-up work." Carrie had laid down the law. It was always her. Dom busied himself with pouring a cup of coffee and dropping two pieces of bread in the toaster.

Jess stormed out of the kitchen without taking a single spoonful of her cereal, which would now soak to sogginess in the bowl left on the table. Sheridan stood up. She had already eaten her cereal. She rinsed the bowl in the sink, and said she would be outside on the front porch, waiting to leave. It was as if she had known Carrie was not happy with Dom, and she hadn't wanted to listen to the argument that could come of it.

"I'll be out there as soon as Jess changes," Carrie spoke.

"Bye honey," Dom added, as he generously buttered the toast on the counter.

Carrie waited for the door to close. "So you bought Jess a shirt. I get that. I also understand if you didn't see her try it on at the store. She may not even have gone into the fitting room. What I don't get is how you could stand here and see how that piece of clothing bared a little too much of your daughter's chest. She's only eleven, and she's going to school for chrissakes!"

Dom took a bite of toast and instantly half of one piece was already gone. He chewed and tried to keep his mouth partially closed as he spoke. "Honey, she's a little girl. I'm not being creepy, but there's nothing there to show off yet."

"That is beside the point. She's out of control. And when I need you to support me, to parent with me, you're oblivious."

"Well, tell me next time. Give me a fair warning and I'll back you up." Dom was now biting into his second piece of toast. He was being agreeable. That's what he did to avoid conflict with her. Carrie was past fed up. Maybe she wanted an argument to turn into a full blown fight. They needed to show some emotion again. Come alive. Feel alive with each other and in their marriage.

"You didn't tell me that you bought new shoes." Carrie was looking for a fight, for sure. She was armed and ready to instigate. "I could have picked up a pair for you, as I have for the past two decades. What prompted you to shop for yourself?"

Dom wiped the toast crumbs from the corners of his mouth with a paper towel and washed his last bite of toast down with more coffee. "Jess and I were hanging out here alone. She suggested we go to the mall. I walked around on my own while she tried on clothes. I ended up in the shoe department." He looked down at his feet, as if he was admiring the loafers. Carrie thought they didn't quite fit Dom's style. He was a big burly man. Those shoes seemed too soft for him. "Do you like them?" He didn't tell her that Rob, the new guy at the office who he hired several months ago, wore a similar pair.

"Yeah, they're okay," she lied. She was aware the tone of her voice was unfeeling.

"Don't start the day off mad, Care." It was as if Dom was offended now. *Over shoes!*

"Mad? Okay, yes, I am upset. We don't communicate. We are lost to each other in this huge house, and you just keep acting like that's fine. Well it's not fine! I want our marriage back." She refrained to mention how he never touched her anymore. Maybe if he had, none of this would seem as dire. Maybe their intimate time together — the time designated for only them when they could shut out the rest of the world — would make up for his long work hours and lack of communication.

Dom, at first, wouldn't make eye contact with her. He remained stationary near the granite countertop, and she had never moved from her chair at the table. "Carrie, I work long hours to give our family all of this," he said, lifting both of his hands into the air. Their kitchen alone had a high, arched ceiling that reached twenty-feet at its peak. They had a kitchen table that seated eight, which was fit for an elegant dining room with high-back cushioned chairs. There were never eight people dining together in that house, with the exception of the girls and their friends — but they seldom used a table to eat.

"Yes, I know," she began, "but for a very long time, all of this," she lifted her hands in the air to mimic him, "hasn't been enough."

They were interrupted when Jess walked back into the kitchen. Carrie glanced at her. There was no skin showing. She had chosen a sweatshirt, similar to her sister's. Jess just stood there. She overheard what her mother said. And this was the first time she had ever wondered if her parents loved each other. There was an obvious tension and distance between them in the room that even an eleven year old could pick up on.

"Sheridan is outside. Join her. I'll be out in a minute."

"Bye honey," Dom repeated to his other daughter this time.

When both of the girls were out of the house, Carrie spoke again. "No late meetings tonight. Cancel them. Clear your ever-so-demanding calendar. We are going to talk after dinner."

She watched Dom open his mouth, as if he was going to object, or perhaps to tell her he had a pertinent business deal on his agenda which needed his immediate attention. It would not have been the first time. But instead, he closed his mouth, stayed silent, and just nodded his head. He never reached for her. Never kissed her goodbye. He only walked past her in the kitchen of their half a million dollar home, and said, "see you tonight."

Carrie blinked back the tears that were now welling up in her eyes.

Chapter Eleven

All sixteen years of Tabitha's nursing career were spent at Hays Medical Center, commonly referred to as HaysMed. She was known there, recognized there as one of the most trusted medical professionals. She loved being a trauma nurse. She thrived during emergencies. She was a think-on-her-feet kind of person and that benefitted her greatly as a professional in an emergent setting. Tabitha had grown up in Hays, which made seeing familiar faces at that local hospital a daily occurrence. Sometimes she wished she wasn't recognized, but most of the time she enjoyed when it was noted that someone knew her by name. There was a trust level which was involuntarily when patients were in need of medical attention and identified the face of the nurse asking the questions and attempting to help.

There was commotion. There was disorder at the entrance of the ER when two men in beer distributer uniforms bolted through the door with a third man propped in the middle of them. His feet were not even touching the floor. Ryker Davis was pale and on the verge of blacking out. That much was obvious, but not nearly as evident as the blood-soaked white towel thickly wrapped around and completely covering one of his hands. Tabitha bolted into the lobby first as soon as she heard one of the men relay in a panic to the receptionist that a co-worker's fingers had been severed. Another man, looking as equally as pale as the victim, held up a clear plastic bag with those fingers on ice. Ryker Davis was immediately planted into a wheelchair. Tabitha instructed another nurse to get him to *Room 2* as she took ahold of the bag and ran alongside of the wheelchair that was rapidly on the move.

"Ryker, hand up. Hold your hand up. Keep it up." She assisted him to sustain his arm in the air to help stem the bleeding. "You know me, right?" Tabitha was checking to be sure he had not gone into shock. Because he, in fact, had known her very well. Ryker worked for Donnewald Beer Distributing in Hays, and he was a life-long best friend of Rory's. The double-R boys. The R-squared men. They had been friends since they were toddlers, living and growing up in the same neighborhood. Ryker was the best man in Tabitha's wedding. He sat at the makeshift poker table in her kitchen for countless all-nighters. She had seen him drunk and passed out on her living room couch. She witnessed him broken-hearted when his fiancé called off their engagement five weeks prior to the wedding. She watched him pick himself up from heartbreak and eventually fall in love again. Ryker was now happily married and a father to two little ones. His boy was two years old and his baby girl was seven months.

Tabitha watched him nod his head of blond hair. It was so blond it could have passed for white. He swallowed hard before he spoke. "Save my fucking fingers." She wanted to laugh, but didn't. She loved Ryker like a brother. And now she would take immediate action to help save his fingers that had been severed when the mechanical lift malfunctioned on the beer truck that he was operating. Tabitha instructed the nurse assisting her to direct pressure on the wound, while she tore into the iced bag. The severed fingers were at risk. The direct contact with the ice could have given the vessels freezer burn. Tabitha realized this was a misconception for people to immediately put a severed body part on ice to save it. That was partly true, but it should be wrapped in a clean cloth first. Tabitha rinsed off the fingers to decrease the bacteria on them before she wrapped them in sterile gauze and inserted that into another bag of ice that was prepared for her. And within minutes, a surgeon in the hospital was on hand and Ryker was placed on a gurney and rushed into the operating room.

Surgically reattaching severed fingers had an eighty-percent success rate, if the feeling returned in them. Most of the correct, timely steps had been taken, and Tabitha was confident that Ryker would see a complete recovery. Even still, she was worried about him. She had taken a break to talk to and offer comfort to his wife, Joann — who they called Jo. She had bolted through the door after they had taken him into surgery. While Tabitha sat with her in the waiting room, she also texted Rory to let him know what was going on. He came there right away. They were brothers. No doubt about it. She watched him hold tight to Jo when he first entered the waiting room. She clung to him and cried in his arms, and Tabitha stood back and felt so adoring and proud of her man. He was loving, caring, and he held all of his cards close. *If he loved you, he took care of you.*

Tabitha was the first person to see Ryker when he was in recovery. She had gone through those personnel only double doors that led to the recovery room designated for surgical patients immediately following their procedures.

He was groggy, but coming out of the anesthetic coma. His wife would be called into that recovery area shortly. "Hey you. Did you lose a couple of digits on the jobsite today?" Tabitha watched him attempt a grin. His clothes had been cut off and he was wearing a hospital gown, which didn't suit a tough, masculine guy like Ryker. The full cheeks on his face were still blood stained in spots. *Blood was squirting everywhere,* one of his coworkers had reported like a typical man willing to tell a good, gory story.

"Just tell me they are reattached, so I won't look like a freak," Ryker replied. His attempt to be funny was overlooked by Tabitha. She knew he was scared.

"Absolutely. HaysMed only has the best of the best. You're going to be fine." Tabitha watched him smile. And then he closed his eyes again. It was time for Tabitha to get his wife in there to see him.

At the end of her shift that evening, Tabitha found the hospital room that Ryker was admitted to. He would be observed at least overnight before he could go home. And then he would have to begin weeks of physical therapy on his hand.

"Thank you for all you've done today," was the first thing Jo said when Tabitha tapped her knuckles on the door and walked into Ryker's assigned room.

"Not me. The surgeon." She never took credit when it wasn't deserving of her.

"Just having you here to take action when he came in, when he was moved to surgery in a rush, and checking on him and me — was a comfort." Jo was grateful.

Tabitha smiled. "I did keep your ass from keeling over when I planted it into that chair on wheels." Ryker laughed out loud, but he was still weak and medicated. The pain and the throbbing in those fingers was going to be extreme for a few days or more.

"Thank Rory for showing up. Jo told me he was here, and waited with her when you had to get back to work. I was still out of it when he left."

"He had to get the boys from school," Tabitha stated. "I'm headed home now to see them. Have you guys eaten? Need anything?"

Jo told her that Ryker's dinner tray was ordered and she planned to grab something from the cafeteria while he ate. Tabitha offered to stay with him while Jo went down to the cafeteria. She knew Jo had been too upset to eat or drink anything while her husband was in surgery. She only weighed a hundred pounds the way it was, so Tabitha insisted she eat.

When they were left alone, Ryker spoke first. "I really scared her."

"Yeah. Asshole."

He chuckled, weakly. "How long am I going to be out of work?"

"What were you told? Has Dr. Gagen been in to see you post surgery?"

"Three to six weeks, depending on my progress. That sucks with Jo not working." His wife was a stay-at-home-mom to their babies, and had planned to be until they reached school age.

"You have insurance, you'll collect workman's compensation. Relax, Ryker. But I get you. I hear you. One-income coming in sucks. I am not one to pinch my pennies. But apparently I am one to work my fingers to the bone."

"Ugh, no. Bad analogy today. Please, no mention of fingers… and bones." Ryker had a look of disgust on his face, and Tabitha giggled. "Rory doesn't talk much about his unemployment. I don't bring it up because I think it makes him uncomfortable."

"He's content doing what he does, which is practically everything around the house. He's there for the boys, and for me. He's a woman's dream husband — he cooks, he cleans, he fixes anything that breaks. Oh and he's incredibly hot in bed."

"Okay, okay!" Ryker held up his good hand to make her stop, as he mostly pretended she had offered too much personal information. It wasn't as if he and his best friend hadn't discussed their sex lives. They always had, and still did. Ryker got serious then. "But he needs to get a job, huh?" Everyone just assumed that Tabitha's salary could carry them without any strife. It could, but her biggest worry was there was no money being saved for their future.

She nodded. "Something has to come up soon."

"But he's picky. He wants to get back into construction, but it will have to be on his terms — and those are some pretty steep terms."

"Yeah, I know, but honestly I just want a paycheck to come in. I know he has his pride, but he's mechanical and so handy, he could do absolutely anything."

"Anything but drive a freaking beer truck..." Ryker stated and he rolled his eyes.

"What?"

"We've been hiring for awhile. At least a half a dozen distributors have come on board in the last month or so. I told Rory. He shrugged it off." Ryker knew he needed to tread lightly with that admission. He actually regretted his words as soon as he saw Tabitha's eyes widen.

"What am I going to do with him?"

"Put him to bed without dinner?" Ryker grinned, mischievously.

"He makes dinner. I'll need him to cook it first." They were joking, but in the back of her mind —no it was front and center now— Tabitha was angry with, and disappointed in, her husband.

Chapter Twelve

After dinner, the girls retreated to their separate bedrooms. They both had speeches to prepare for the end the week in their sixth grade English class, and neither one of them had chosen a topic yet. They had three days to prepare, plan, and finish. Carrie sent them upstairs to research, even if it took them the rest of the night. She was short with them and irritable, and they both had noticed. Neither one of them, even Jess, had attempted to question or defy her. Jess had shared with her twin that she had walked in on the tail-end of a fight or a conversation that was way too serious between their parents. *I think they are going to get a divorce.* Sheridan had retorted that she was being *ridiculous.*

After the dishwasher was loaded, Carrie found Dom in his office. It was equivalent to a library, or a den, on the main level of their house. He had a desk, a computer, a copy and fax machine, and book shelves lined two of the four walls. He was a reader of anything nonfiction. Dom soaked up knowledge any chance he got.

"Is this a good place for us to talk?" she asked, stepping through the open doorway without awaiting his response. She wanted his full attention. His mind was on work enough. She walked on the frayed ends of her flared light denim in bare feet. Her black turtleneck sweater was loose and baggy fitting. Her blonde curls were stuck to the folded over, high neck of her sweater. He had a rocking chair positioned near one of the book shelves, and Carrie sat down on it and curled her legs underneath her.

The fact that she wanted to talk had taken him aback, and it kept crossing his mind and haunting him all day long. He wondered how serious she would be with her words. *Would she cry? Give him an ultimatum? Force him to open up?* Dom was still wearing his black suit pants, white shirt, and his red tie was loosened around his neck. He had taken off his loafers earlier and now crossed his ankles underneath his desk with only black socks on his feet. He removed the wire rimmed glasses that were resting on the end of his nose, and he turned his large leather chair toward his wife.

"Dom, I know I'm not overacting or imagining things. We have drifted so far apart that I don't recognize us anymore. This isn't who we are. We both know that because we have a baseline to compare then and now to. We were once good together. We loved each other passionately. We had fun together. I want that back. Help me to find that again. Meet me halfway." She practically said all of that in one breath. She talked nonstop, and fast, whenever she was nervous.

"Carrie… life changes. We are busier, older…"

"Wealthier," she added.

"You think money has changed me?"

"I think you work too hard."

"Look what we have," he again held up his hands as he had in their kitchen earlier this morning. It was as if he thought his wife needed to be reminded that she lived in a castle — thanks to him.

"And look what we've lost along the way," she added, sadly.

"You're an artist, a successful one at that. You have your gallery, your studio. We have two healthy, beautiful girls that we are raising together. We can afford new cars for them when they turn sixteen. Their college funds are in place. We have so much to be grateful for."

"I agree. But what about us? Remember you and me? Someday the girls will be grown with lives of their own. We will be old and retired. And it will be just us in this house, sharing the same world day in and day out. I can't seem to get a decent conversation out of you now. What then? Disconnected lives under the same roof? Separate beds?"

"I know it's been a really long time since we've —" Dom paused. He was clearly uncomfortable.

"Had sex? Made love? Touched each other?" Those words never used to be a source of embarrassment or awkwardness between them. This was a man who she used to lay naked beside, shower with. He knew every inch of her. Had ravished all of her. "What's wrong, Dom? Is it me? Jesus. I've always been chubby. You never made me feel anything but comfortable, sexy, and beautiful. What has changed?" Carrie thought she saw tears well up in his eyes. She stood up from the rocker, and padded slowly in her bare feet, over to him.

She was still sexy and beautiful to him. She always would be. He just needed to find a way to be able to tell her that again. And show her. It just felt so impossible right now. Because, she was right, he had changed. His feelings were confusing, and even frightening to him at times. He was a man of prestige and honor. He loved his wife and their family. He wasn't someone who gave up or gave in. Not for anything.

He reached for her. He gripped both of his hands in hers. Carrie immediately noticed him trembling. "I'm sorry," he spoke. "I want to fix this. You're my wife. Mine. I don't want to lose you, or us, or the family we've created and shared all these years."

This was a start. Carrie felt the tears rolling down her cheeks. He stood up to her, towered her, and took her face in both of his hands now. He kissed her eagerly, full and hard on the mouth. She responded with the same desire she always had for this man. But his longing was different toward her. There was no intensity to his touch, his kisses. And Carrie squeezed her eyes shut tight when she realized it felt forced and obligated on his end. She wanted this chance though. To start over. To try again. And her body had ached for this for far too long. There was a maroon-colored leather sectional against the far wall of the den. He took her body with his there. She forced herself to open her eyes, not to shut out how different it felt. How foreign he felt in her arms. But when her eyes were open, she saw that his were closed. It was almost as if he was somewhere else. Thinking of something, or someone, else. And with his release, she saw he was crying.

"I think there's someone else. Dom could be cheating on me." Carrie had summoned Tabitha to her studio. It was ten o'clock that night, four hours after she and Dom had *reunited* in his den. Carrie was relieved to know that Tabitha didn't have to work in the morning. It was her day off as she already had worked three consecutive twelve-hour shifts in the ER again.

"Oh my God, Carrie." Tabitha reached for her hand and held it as they sat together on the old cherry red sofa in her studio. "What happened to make you think that now?"

"I confronted him about our marriage not being the same, our lack of communication, closeness, all of it. He seemed genuine when he said he wanted to work on all of that. He wanted me, our girls, our family, and our life together. I believed him. He's not a liar."

"But he's a cheater? If he's cheating on you, he's lying to you. Do you know for sure?"

"No, I don't know for sure. We had sex in his den."

"Oh? Finally!"

"Yes, finally. But Tab, I'm telling you, it was different. It was off. He felt off. We felt disconnected even though we were together in the complete sense."

"So you think his mind was somewhere else, on someone else maybe?"

"Maybe," Carrie repeated Tabitha's *maybe*, because it was easier not to say, or know, for certain.

"Oh honey…"

"This sucks so bad," Carrie stated, and she felt like crying.

"Either confront him or follow him." Tabitha was serious.

"I think I like the latter idea best."

Chapter Thirteen

The twins were at volleyball practice, and Carrie had two hours before she needed to be their chauffer again. Tonight she was going to skip going back to her studio to paint. Dom texted her that he had a late meeting, which meant not to hold dinner for him, and typically he made it home before the girls had to be in their bedrooms with the lights out and phones off. Carrie took a drive downtown. Dom's car was parked in the lot across the street from his office. She parked adjacent to it. The entire fifth floor of the building was well-lit. Carrie parked and got out of her SUV. She was prepared to use a key to unlock the door that led to the main lobby of the building. She had taken that key off of Dom's key ring two days ago. He must not have missed it, because he had not said anything to her about it. The only time he used that key was when he went back to the office after he had been home for dinner, or on the weekends. He had not needed it since Carrie stole it, and tonight she planned to use it.

She walked across the street, after waiting for cars in both directions. It was dark, and she felt criminal-like, as if she was breaking and entering into a building she had only been in twice since she married Dom fifteen years ago. She didn't even know what she would say to her husband when she saw him. In the back of her mind, Carrie believed he would be the one caught in the act. She was certain he had a sexy secretary who he was screwing on top of his desk every night. Carrie felt somewhat out of control in her thoughts right now. And sadly, she reminded herself of Beth. This was different, though, Carrie believed, because she was not going to fight and claw to keep Dom — if he was indeed cheating on her. She didn't want him anymore. They had gone back to being who they were after they were intimate in his den a few nights ago. They hardly communicated since, and sex had not been initiated by either of them again. They hadn't begun to find their way back to each other. Not in the least.

Carrie encountered no one in the lobby or on her way up in the elevator to the fifth floor. When the elevator door opened, she crossed paths with a man she recognized as Steve. He seemed in a rush to leave, and Carrie didn't care to talk at the moment either. They exchanged friendly hellos, and Steve told her that *Dom was in his office*. The main secretary's desk was vacant. Only a few of the offices were occupied, some of the doors were open — and when she reached Dom's office door she saw that it was closed. She wouldn't knock. She wouldn't give him time to prepare. Time to cover up. She looked down at the black peep-toe booties she was wearing with flared light-washed denim. She noticed a paint splatter on the oversized v-neck coral sweater she wore. She hadn't changed out of the clothes she had worn to the gallery and in the studio all day.

She had not thought to polish her toenails. They were colorless and pale. Dom never had been a man to need a woman with flare. But maybe now he did? Carrie wondered if she should have tried harder to keep herself in shape, to turn his head more often, year after year. That wasn't fair though. Dom had let himself go, too. He had too much fat around his middle. His hair had thinned and grayed. They were aging in sync and accepting it — together. She ceased her thoughts. There was no turning back. She turned the handle and opened the door.

"Carrie?" Dom stood up abruptly from behind his desk. He wondered how she got into the building after hours, if he had missed a text or call from her to alert him of something that happened, or of her being on her way there.

Carrie stepped into his office. Another businessman, probably at least ten years younger than her husband, remained casually seated at the corner of Dom's desk. None of this appeared formal to Carrie. Their suit coats were off, their ties were loosened. There were no digital or paper files being pored over. They actually had carry-out containers of food in front of them. Dom was eating dinner with a co-worker. Maybe she was wrong to come there. To suspect him of anything other than working overtime.

"Hi, sorry to interrupt," she looked at her husband and then at the other man.

"Is everything alright with the girls?" Dom instantly pressed her, and he seemed tense.

"Oh gosh, yes they are fine and at volleyball practice right now. I really feel foolish barging in like this, but I was just hoping to surprise you and whisk you away for dinner and some alone time," Carrie lied. She also realized she was not properly dressed or prepared at all to be going out to dinner with her husband — in a suit and tie.

"Oh," Dom seemed to relax some. "Well we are having dinner, a dinner meeting, right now."

"I can see that," Carrie spoke, and she watched the other man stand up from the corner of Dom's desk. She still felt incredibly foolish.

"This is my wife, Carrie. And Carrie, this is Robert, one of our newest and most influential investment analysts in this firm." The polite and business-like Dom had surfaced.

"Oh stop, Dominic," the gentleman responded, appearing utterly flattered. Carrie accepted his hand when he offered it to her. He was almost too graceful in the way he embraced hers and prepared to shake it — too affectionate for a man. She looked down and saw that he wore dressy loafers. Loafers, which were very similar to the new ones Dom had just purchased and worn constantly since. Rob's were snakeskin though. *Flashy*.

Carrie was worldly. She had not lived a sheltered life. She had friends and acquaintances from all walks of life. She loved, and never judged or ridiculed anyone for being different. In fact, Carrie was often drawn to unique or odd. She liked the black sheep, the eccentrics, the loners, the lost. She believed they had the most beautiful souls. This seemed so strange to her right now though. This man, obviously gay, felt like a threat to her. *Ridiculous!* She pushed away that thought. She was ashamed of herself.

"It's wonderful to meet you, Carrie. Dominic has told me oodles of things about you and your beautiful daughters." *Oodles?* Robert's hair was jet black, and thickly gelled with product. He was lean. Clean shaven. And his eyes were deep blue.

"Very nice to meet you as well, Robert."

"Oh please, call me Rob."

Carrie nodded, and caught Dom's eye. "I should go," she said to him. "Next time I will call you. No surprises." Both men laughed in unison. And Dom walked her to the door. He placed his hand on the small of her back, and she heard him say, "See you at home, honey."

He didn't feel like her husband to her right now. The man she lived with and loved for well over a decade should have gone out of his way to make her feel comfortable in an uneasy situation. She meant to surprise him, or so she had said, but she left feeling awkward. She left believing she had interrupted something. And it felt so strange knowing she may have.

The door to Dom's office was sealed tight. Carrie wondered if she turned around and pressed her ear to the solid wood, what would she hear? What were they saying to each other, or about her? Or, had they truly resumed a dinner meeting? The meal looked formal, maybe three course, as Carrie had thought she noticed soup, salad, pasta, and some sort of beef that Robert had been cutting with a knife. Where was the notion of heating up something unhealthy in the office microwave before or after a late-night meeting?

When Carrie took the elevator back down to the lobby, Dom was pacing in his office. "This had to have looked weird to my wife," he spoke, with perspiration pooling above his brow.

"It's dinner between business associates," Rob spoke in their defense. He was not concerned with keeping secrets. He had nothing to hide.

"She's my wife. She's smart and extremely perceptive." Dom stopped pacing when Rob stood toe-to-toe with him. Rob reached with a folded handkerchief in his hand to dab the sweat beads from Dom's forehead.

"I'm not going to tell you what you need to do," Rob spoke, gently, as if he was speaking to a child. "Eventually though, you owe it to her, and to yourself, and to me, to be honest."

"I'm not ready. You know there's so much I can't even explain to myself yet. I can't begin to put this into words. I don't know what I want, long-term. I've never hid that fact from you." Dom was beginning to relax, having Rob in such close proximity to him.

"I understand. I am not asking you for anything. I'm just enjoying this. You. Me. Us." Rob, only about an inch shorter than Dom, pulled him close and kissed him lightly on the lips. Dom responded. His wife was out of the building by now. He was able to completely relax and give in. He succumbed to the feelings that shell shocked him when they surfaced several months ago. It was freeing, exciting, and so new. But he realized the path he was on was going to be utterly destructive to the only life he knew — with his wife and daughters. *Clear your mind,* he heard Robert say to him. *Deep, cleansing breaths. Focus on how you feel. And only what you feel. Right here. And right now.*

Dom closed his eyes, as he stood tall near one corner of his desk in that fifth floor office. Robert had already unfastened Dom's belt, and then his pants, as he bent to his knees in front of him.

Carrie wasn't the submissive type. She wasn't going to be the good wife, who obeyed her husband once he shooed her away. Just moments ago, she had taken the elevator back up to the fifth floor. She had carefully made her way back to that closed office door with Dom and *another man* on the other side of it. She had quietly turned the handle again, and slightly cracked the door. She heard some of their conversation. And that's when she saw their kiss. She brought her hand up to her mouth, and held it there tightly. She was terribly afraid to make a sound. And the tears began to roll down her face as she made herself watch. She never stepped back. She wouldn't run away. She didn't close her eyes. She forced herself to appallingly stare at her husband receiving pleasure from another man. It was like watching two strangers. Gay men. It was pornographic. It was like a car accident scene that she could not look away from, no matter how hard she tried. That man was not her husband. She no longer recognized him. The hurt and confusion that she felt right now was beyond comprehendible. *Her life was over.*

And for the first time ever, she may have understood why Beth did what she did. There were hopeless, helpless outcomes that consumed all reason.

Chapter Fourteen

Tabitha kept quiet about Ryker's admission. Rory had multiple chances — with just one company — to get a job. He just didn't want to work. That had to be it. He enjoyed his freedom to be there for the boys, and to take care of the meals and their household. He was a house-husband and stay-at-home-dad. And that's what he wanted to be.

Right now, he was mowing the grass in their yard. Tabitha could hear the roar of the mower as she sat on their bed with the laptop placed in front of her. Last month, when she checked the balance in their checking account, they had $528 after she was paid her salary from the hospital and practically all of that money went toward paying off their monthly bills. She was due to receive another deposit from the hospital at the end of the week, but that minimal balance in their account worried her. They used their debit card since for everything including groceries, gasoline, and Tabitha had gotten another mani-pedi over the weekend. *She needed one, sure. But she didn't really have to have it.*

She typed in her password, DoubleDmom. She and Rory had gotten a good laugh out of that and its reference to Dillon and Dane, not her breasts — which were every bit of a full C cup. Tabitha looked twice at the new balance on the screen. There was $2,200.47 listed.

"That can't be right…" she said aloud, and alone, in her bedroom. She could still hear the roar of the mower, as Rory had moved to the backyard now. "Where the hell did that money come from?" She stood up from the bed, and paced a few times at the foot of it. She knelt down on the carpeted floor, and pulled the computer closer to her again. The deposit was listed as a *personal deposit; i.e. cash.* Tabitha knew it wasn't her, so it had to be Rory. And now she speculated how he could have come up with that amount of cash.

She closed the laptop, and tucked it underneath her arm. Once in the kitchen, she placed it on top of the island, and then walked out of the back door. The sun was shining, and a warm wind met her directly in the face as her boat shoes stepped onto the freshly cut grass. Rory's back was to her, and she waited for him to turn and begin mowing a new row before he looked up. He killed the motor when he saw her.

"Hey, what's up?" Rory asked her with a smile. *That smile.*

"Just doing some banking online. I have the laptop up in the kitchen, why don't you come take a look at something with me." Rory didn't hesitate to follow her back inside.

He grabbed a bottle of water from the refrigerator and chugged it down as Tabitha sat on a stool near the island. She turned the screen toward him when he set the empty plastic water bottle on the edge of the kitchen sink. "I'm due for a paycheck at the end of the week. Last month, after my check was deposited, and after all of our bills were taken care of, there was a measly $528 balance. I know that dwindled since then, so I logged on to check to see how dangerously close we were to zero." Rory moved closer to the screen. "Did you make that cash deposit?" she asked him. "There's over two thousand in our account now."

Rory backed up from the screen, and made direct eye contact with his wife. "Yes, I did. I sold my dirt bike."

"You did? Why? To who?" This instantly pained her to know. That old Suzuki DR-350 dirt bike, designed for both off-road and on, had been his since he was a nineteen years old. Tabitha could still remember how it felt to sit close behind him, wrap her arms around his waist, and cruise the open roadway. For their first date, he had arrived on that bike to pick her up. She still laughed at that memory. And whenever Tabitha saw that old dirt bike tucked into the corner of their garage, it always made her smile. It was their history, a part of their love story. And now Rory had sold it, without even consulting her. That old dirt bike was gone. It wasn't his to claim anymore.

"I sold it to the guy who opened the Meyer's pool last week." The Meyers had been Rory and Tabitha's neighbors, directly across the street, since the day they moved in to their house a dozen years ago. "It was a nice day, I had the garage open, and I rolled it out to start her up and let her run for a bit. He came walking over when he saw me, or heard the bike. He knew exactly the make, model, and year. He's a collector. He asked me if I would consider selling it." At first, Rory had flat out told him *absolutely no way.* And then he thought about the money he could make. The cash he could contribute to his family. He chose taking care of his family over a treasured possession of his that held many memories.

"Oh my God, Rory... Why didn't you tell me?"

"I guess because I knew you would be upset, just like I was. But, it's okay, it was just a bike."

"Yeah, just a bike with a lot of special memories for us. I was sitting on it when you kissed me for the first time."

Rory nodded his head. "I know, I remember..."

"Dammit, Rory! Fucking ask me next time!" Tabitha felt hot tears welling up in her eyes. He looked down at his feet on the floor. He hadn't taken off his grass-mowing shoes. The once white soles of those tennis shoes were completely green, and there were grass clippings stuck to them. Some had fallen off onto the cream-colored tiled flooring.

Rory looked at her solemnly. "Well, $1,900 sure wasn't worth the look on your face right now." He walked over to her, and he pulled her close. She reached her arms around him and held him tightly.

"The money helps, okay?" she admitted. "But don't ever do something like that again. Not without talking to me first. Got it?"

"You're kind of sexy when you're bossy..."

"Stop it. I mean it. And you have to get a job. We can't live without any savings, emergency money, or just everyday spending money for chrissakes."

"I'll get serious. I'll check with Ryker. I know Donnewald was hiring." *Was*, Tabitha thought. "I guess it's time for me to quit being particular. But, you know, Tab, things will change around here. The boys are going to have to take the bus to school. There will be no more home-cooked meals on the table every night after your long shifts at the hospital."

"We can manage. We have to, Rory." Tabitha wondered if he was trying to talk her out of his going back to work.

"I know," he said, but his tone had not sounded convincing to Tabitha. "But first, the grass." Rory started to walk away, to go back outside.

"I'm running out for awhile. I'll be at the gym, and then I'm stopping for groceries." She was out of wine again, but had not dared to say as much. If she had a bottle now, she would pour herself a full glass — and yes it was still morning.

"That gym membership isn't cheap, Tab."

"It's something I don't want to give up," she told him.

"And you think I wanted to give up my dirt bike!" Before she could answer him, he abruptly walked out of the kitchen and slammed the back door of the house behind him. It rattled on the hinges. She had almost forgotten how Rory handled stress. He didn't. He lost his temper a lot. He was short with the boys, and especially with her.

She wore layered tank tops, one hot pink and one black, with cropped black leggings. Her caramel brown hair with blonde highlights was pulled back and up high on her head. She intended to drive straight to the gym. She changed her clothes and left without telling Rory she was headed out and would return later, probably in time for lunch. She picked up her phone while she drove out of their neighborhood. And she sent Carrie a quick text.

Are you at the gallery already?

Yes.

Can I come by?

Yes, but be warned, I'm in an awful mood.

Tabitha was caught off guard by Carrie's response. She dropped her phone into the cup holder in the counsel between the car seats, and she pressed her foot down on the gas pedal.

Carrie wiped the tears from her eyes in front of the mirror that hung over the sink in the tiny bathroom of her studio. She then called through the doorway that led to the gallery. "Sharon… my friend Tabitha will be here soon. Just send her back, please." Sharon was used to manning the customers and the sales at the gallery. Most days Carrie needed to be creative, without interruption, in her studio. Dealing with customers inevitably got to be too much, so Carrie had hired Sharon to be her customer service. She was a retired teacher's aide who Carrie had met at the girls' grade school in Hays a few years back.

She stood in front of 'The Trip Not Taken' painting. She hadn't painted much on it the last couple of days. Not since the night she found out that her husband was keeping a dreadful secret. Living a double life was actually how Carrie perceived it. And she had told Dom as much when he came home from the office the very same night she had spied him with *Rob.* That image, burned forever in her memory now, had left her feeling sickened and broken.

Carrie had given the girls permission to see a late movie on a school night. They had been asking her for months to let them see a Thursday night thriller with their friends. Another mom was going to drive them to and from the theater. Their speech projects had been completed, and Carrie suggested that they go to the movies. Both of the girls knew something was strange about their mother's impulsive offer, but neither one of them had asked her what was wrong. Not even Sheridan, because she feared that Jess was right. *Their parents' marriage was in trouble.*

Dom pulled into the garage at eight-thirty. The movie had started at eight, and Carrie was not expecting the girls to be home until a few minutes after ten o'clock. She was waiting for him upstairs in their bedroom when he had come up there looking for someone at home in their quiet house. She heard him push open the doors to the girls' rooms before he entered theirs. She was seated on the ivory sofa.

"Oh, there you are. Where are the girls this late?"

"The movies."

Dom stared hard at her. Something was amiss. He assumed she was embarrassed or disappointed that he could not take part in her impromptu plans. She never stopped by his office. Ever. He had been caught completely off guard. He felt on edge again being in her presence.

"Hey, about tonight… I'm really sorry that I was in the middle of a dinner meeting. If I had known—"

"A dinner meeting? Hmm. Yeah it looked real professional between you two." Carrie's tone was cold. And Dom was well aware of how her jaw clenched and her eyes bore into his.

"Rob is very serious about his job," Dom caught himself defending him. "He's all about fine dining, too, so if you're referring to the elaborate carry-out order we had, that's just him. He's never used a microwave in his life." Dom let out a nervous chuckle.

"It seems that you know quite a lot about Rob. You like his style? I saw the matching shoes." *And so much more.*

Dom didn't respond to her comment. He just slipped off those loafers she had referred to, and stated, "I'm going to shower, and try to stay awake until the girls get home."

"Remember how we used to keep each other awake at night?" Carrie asked him, not taking her eyes off of her husband, standing so far from her, entirely across their bedroom. There was so much distance between them now. What Dom had done would permanently sever the two of them. Their marriage was over. He stared back, and she watched him uncomfortably loosen his deep blue tie. "I could give you a blowjob..."

Carrie stood up and walked slowly toward him. She saw him tense up. Oddly, he touched his hand to his belt buckle. She was toe to toe with him, just as she had seen him and Rob through the narrow wedge she had formed between the door and its frame. "I haven't seen your eyes roll back like that in a very long time. Or heard your pleasure moans. You used to run your fingers through my hair too." There were tears streaming down her face, and the look on Dom's face was pure devastation.

"Oh God... Carrie."

"No, actually, it was, Oh God, Robbie!" she spat at him through her tears. He stepped back from her and ran his large hands, all of his fingers, through his short cropped gray hair. "All these months, you never touched me. You're not a cheat, I told myself. You're just a busy man, you're tired at the end of a long work day. We drifted apart, and I thought we needed to remind each other of who we used to be. We made love in your den, but I couldn't shake the feeling of something being off. You felt different to me. You rushed the way you touched me. You were fighting in your mind to displace yourself, to imagine yourself somewhere else. I thought then that you had another woman and you were screwing her. Prettier. Thinner. Much younger. But no, it's a man you want. A man to suck your dick!" Carrie let out a sob, so hard that she almost choked on her saliva. Dom reached for her, and she shoved him away with both of her palms on his thick, broad, chest. He backed up two or three more steps from her. He had tears on his face now, too.

"I never wanted it to come to this," he began. His face was flushed. His eyes were obviously pained. "I am a man. I have always been into women, you, your body. I mean it, God I mean it. I never thought about or had any of those kinds of feelings. But I started to have them for Rob. We worked together closely. He was openly gay. He talked about it, himself, his experience — like nothing. I pushed, no, I shoved away those thoughts that I started to have. I fought them. I swear I did. I was confused and disgusted with myself. And then Rob saw through me. He called me out. And I relented. He started trying things with me...and I allowed him to."

"Jesus Christ, Dom! Don't you think it's bad enough that I saw it? Now you're going to speak in detail too!" Carrie used her fingers to wipe the tears from her face in annoyance. *She wouldn't cry over him. He repulsed her.*

"I just want you to know that I will stop. Nothing like that will happen again. From the beginning, I've told Rob that it's no-strings-attached. I can turn it off. I want my life with you and our girls."

Carrie laughed at him. Her chuckle sounded borderline evil. "Do you hear yourself? What you are saying is unbelievably preposterous! You want to fuck someone else and still come home to play the honorable husband and father here?"

"No! No! I'm done. I said that I would stop. It's over! Please hear me on this."

"No, you hear me! Take your loafers and your stiff dick somewhere else. Just get out! I can't even look at you anymore…" Carrie turned her back. Her throat was sore from screaming. She refused to circle back around to look at him. But she heard him loud and clear.

"This is my house. Those girls are mine. Your painting hobby will only carry you so far down the street. Good luck with that." And then he left their bedroom to take a shower.

Carrie stood there, trembling in place. She had thoughts of calling a divorce attorney right then and there. She refused to pack her bags. She was not leaving without her daughters. What Dom did was grounds for her to profit excessively in a divorce settlement. But what she ended up doing was nothing. She slept on the sofa in their bedroom that night, or rather, she laid there with her eyes closed, wondering what her next move would be. Existing there, living a lie with him, while she could never trust him again, was not an option.

When Tabitha's tennis shoes stepped onto one of the paint-splattered bare floorboards, it creaked. Carrie had been so far gone, into her thoughts, until then. "Oh goodness, I never even heard you come in."

Tabitha took one look at her dearest friend left in this world, and she knew something was very wrong. Her blonde curls had not been combed, or styled at all. Her faded jeans and oversized white t-shirt were wrinkled as if she had worn them for days and slept in them overnight. Her face was makeup-less, her skin was blotchy red, and her eyes were teary. "Honey, what's wrong?"

That's all it took for the floodgates to open. Carrie spent the next few minutes sobbing in her arms. She was certain her sudden and uncontrollable burst of emotion had echoed and was heard by Sharon in the gallery up front.

Tabitha grabbed ahold of her firmly by the shoulders. "It's Dom. He's cheating on you. You know for sure now, don't you?" Tabitha watched Carrie nod her head, and Tabitha's response was, "Bastard!"

"I took your suggestion and I followed him, or rather I just showed up at his office when was working late," Carrie began. "I expected to find a hot little secretary bent over his desk. Little did I know." Tabitha waited for Carrie to continue. "Dom was in the middle of a dinner with another businessman from his firm. It all looked strange from the moment I walked in. Fancy food. Their relaxed nature at first glance before Dom immediately got nervous around me — and Rob."

"Who's Rob?"

"A new guy at the office, since several months ago. He wears snakeskin loafers, overly gels his hair, and his handshake is entirely too gentle."

"So he's gay?" Tabitha concluded.

"That he is. And it seems he's convinced my husband to play for the other team as well…"

"Oh my God! You are kidding me? This is insane. You're going to have to explain this to me. Big, burly, Dom?" Tabitha's ongoing rant was expected, and Carrie had initially felt all of the same emotions and still had those unanswered questions.

"Dom rushed me out of the office that night. I just felt so strange being there with the two of them. Rob was calm and cordial. Dom was the complete opposite. I left, I took the elevator down to the lobby. But then I went right back. I cracked open his office door to listen. I heard enough to know that Dom has conflicted feelings, and I saw more than my share to conclude that my husband prefers a man to manipulate his dick."

Tabitha's hand flew to her mouth. Her eyes widened. "You saw them?"

"It was not your classic blowjob. Not hardly when you watch another man *with* your husband."

"What he has done to you is sick! You kicked him to the curb, right?" Tabitha was livid.

"He was beyond apologetic. He admitted his confusion about these new feelings. He said it's over with Rob. He wants to go on like it never happened. He also told me in no uncertain terms that if I choose to leave him, I will never make it with my measly paintings, and our girls will stay with him."

"He's not going to get away with that!" Tabitha blurted out. "No judge would fail to see your side of this. You will get what Dom is worth."

"I know that. If he thinks just because I'm laying low, that I'm slowly getting over this, then he's dead wrong. I just needed some time to gather my strength and find myself the best damn divorce attorney in Kansas."

"We are going to do that today. Right here. Right now." Carrie watched Tabitha retrieve her phone. She obviously was about to begin her research on Google.

Carrie stepped away, and toward the mini refrigerator in the corner. "I need alcohol."

"Amen." Tabitha wholeheartedly agreed.

Chapter Fifteen

Rory received Tabitha's text stating she would not be home for lunch because she was dealing with a crisis with Carrie. He showered after mowing then, and left the house in search of a job that he was in no hurry to find. He drove past Donnewald twice before he finally gave in and turned into the main lot. He thought about calling Ryker first, but he was still on medical leave while he recovered from the on-site injury to his hand. If anything, Rory thought he could list Ryker's name as a reference if he went inside and filled out an application for a job. He sat in his truck and waited. Waited for the courage to go inside and admit that he was looking for work. A grown man and jobless at forty years old. He was hardly a failure, but doing this certainly made him feel like one.

He cracked the tinted window near him and sunk down in the driver's seat. Then he killed the engine to conserve the gasoline in the tank. Money for everything was obviously tight these days, as Tabitha continued to emphasize to him. He sat there for awhile before he noticed activity in the lot. One of the distribution trucks had just pulled in and parked near the main building. Rory watched a tall, dark haired, broad-shouldered man climb down from the truck. He recognized him immediately as Joe Morgan. *The man who Beth lost her mind over.* Rory still couldn't believe the freakish nature of that story. *What an awful way to take your own life*, everyone had reiterated, all over the City of Hays, no matter where he went for weeks on end. Many people knew Rory's connection to Beth as she was his wife's best friend. *One, among the trio of girls, who were the inseparable friends from college.*

Rory watched the arrogant son of a bitch swagger as he walked. He held in his hand what resembled an insulated stainless steel Yeti cup. Another car pulled into the lot just as he was walking around to the back end of the distribution truck. The car parked one over from being nose to nose with Rory's truck. His truck windows were tinted, but obviously not his windshield, so Rory stayed low in his seat. He watched Joe Morgan walk toward the car. A man in dark sunglasses stepped out. Joe shook his hand. And then Rory saw him give the man in sunglasses the Yeti. In turn, Joe Morgan was handed an obvious, significant wad of cash. This was a drug deal in the daylight, out there in the open lot of a public business. Rory was alarmed. Joe Morgan walked off, and a second later the car backed out and drove away.

Rory considered his options. He could call the police, or call Ryker to find out the name of the top boss inside to rat out Joe Morgan. Or, he could stay out of it altogether. Because, after all, Joe Morgan was a dangerous man. In Beth's honor though, Rory felt compelled to do something. He sat up taller behind the steering wheel of his truck now, and that's when he noticed Joe Morgan staring back at him. He was standing near the open backend of the distribution truck, and he clearly had his eyes on Rory. Rory also realized Joe Morgan knew that no vehicles had come or gone into the lot since *his deal* occurred. So he had known Rory saw it.

He stepped toward Rory's truck. Rory contemplated turning over the engine and getting out of there. But he didn't. He had done nothing wrong. But Joe Morgan certainly had.

Rory stepped out as Joe Morgan approached him. If anything, he would slam his truck door and carry on with his initial plan to fill out a job application inside of the main building. "Rory. Good to see you again. Can I help you with something here?" Joe Morgan of course placed Rory immediately. Beth had thrown the six of them together as couples at least twice. His voice was deep and husky, and he towered Rory by about four inches.

"No, I've got it all under control. Just looking to get hired, and going inside to inquire about that." Rory, annoyed with himself, wondered why he offered so much information.

"Yeah, I heard your construction gig folded after bankruptcy. That's been awhile though. Time to find some work, huh?"

He nodded. "Yep." He started to step away, but Joe Morgan blocked him. "I won't keep you," Rory told him, making another attempt to move on.

"I just had a thought," Joe Morgan offered. Rory listened. "You could work for me."

Rory inhaled a deep breath through his nostrils, and replied, "I told you, I'm about to go inside to see about applying."

Joe Morgan shook his head. "Rory Chance, I am aware of enough about you to know you're street smart. You saw the exchange through your windshield just now. It's side money. I don't use opioid. I just deal. Easy money, man. For you, there can still be no eight-hour work days. No boss-man to answer to. You can still do what you do — only difference will be money in the bank. You know, get the wife off your back."

"Leave my wife out of this," Rory fumed.

"We can, sure we can. Just fabricate a means for the money coming in."

Rory shook his head. "I'm not into crime."

"And neither am I." There was confidence and insistency in Joe Morgan's voice. It was almost frightening — even to another grown man.

"I said, I have to go," Rory told him, and pushed past him this time.

"Chance!" His voice forced Rory to turn around and face him out there in the blustery wind. "Advanced pay right this second will be two grand. A location, day or night, your preference, to hand off a Yeti in exchange for cash, can happen as early as tomorrow. That's how this works. So, the way I see it, you have two choices. Take my offer, or walk up to the main desk in there and tuck your dick between your legs to apply for a measly paying job. There's no money for the low man starting here."

"You forgot my third choice," Rory boldly spoke up. "I could take your job. You know, the one you will no longer have once your underground dealing out here comes to light and you will not only lose your job, but your freedom."

Rory watched Joe Morgan smirk and then repeatedly nod his head. "Right… you're that brave of a boy, are you? Well you do that, and I'll see to it that your wife has not seen the last of me." Rory clenched his jaw, and then both of his fists. "Yeah, Elizabeth got awfully hung up on me. They were close friends, had the same interests. I could show your wife some of my charm…"

Rory lunged toward him, but Joe Morgan was quicker and he grabbed ahold of him by the neck with both of his massive, strong hands. "You're an idiot!" Rory scoffed at him, and attempted to physically fight him off. He wasn't going to succumb to defeat. "There has to be cameras out here."

"You think I don't know where those cameras are?" Joe Morgan threw those words back at him. He released his grip of him, and then he reached into the front pocket of his cotton grayish-blue pants that were a part of his beer distributor uniform. He forcefully stuffed a wad of cash into the front pocket of Rory's denim. "I own you now. You work for me. I'll be in touch about your first obligation. And remember, if you go to the cops, I'll go to your wife."

Rory was trembling uncontrollably when he got back behind the wheel of his truck again. For the first time in his life, he knew exactly what it felt like to be a coward. He had dirty money on him. *If anything ever happened to Tabitha, he would lose his mind. How could he protect her from a man like Joe Morgan?* It was too dangerous not to follow this path. And it was equally as risky to be on it. But Rory believed there was no other choice.

Chapter Sixteen

Rory left the wad of cash tucked inside the front pocket of his denim. He was afraid to touch it, or move it from there to anywhere else. He didn't feel right to spend it, and if he deposited it in the bank, Tabitha obviously would know considering how she regularly kept a close watch online of their dwindling bank account.

He walked into the house, in the kitchen, to find his wife still in her workout clothes. She never made it to the gym this morning, and Rory remembered her text about Carrie in crisis.

"Hi," Tabitha said, hoping their hours apart had done them both some good. And maybe for the rest of the day they could stop talking about money, and teetering on the edge of another argument focused on his lack of interest in job searching. She was just about to pour herself a glass of wine, but was now relieved she hadn't. After spending most of her day off with Carrie, Tabitha had a renewed appreciation for Rory as her faithful, trustworthy husband. He was unlike Dom in so many ways. And for that Tabitha was grateful.

"Hey," Rory spoke. He could feel his heart pounding inside of his chest. He feared the trouble he was in, but even more — he was terrified of being honest and putting Tabitha in any kind of danger. Rory would rather die first, than to ever see her hurt. He wanted to protect her, but he didn't want to lie to her. Not about something this huge.

"I'm sorry," Tabitha offered, moving toward him and into his arms. He held her with a mounting intensity that he couldn't control. He didn't want to let her go. He never wanted to leave their house. *To hell with the rest of the world. He only wanted his wife and his boys. Forever.* Tabitha immediately picked up on the eagerness of his embrace. It was, at first, over-whelming. But she hugged him back, hard, in return, before she wiggled out of his grip. "I spent most of the day with Carrie. She's hurting. Dom did something unforgivable, and she needs an attorney."

"What?" Rory tried to focus on someone else's troubles, instead of his own brewing. "She wants a divorce?"

Tabitha nodded her head. "He's cheating,"

"I told you that was likely the case," Rory stated.

"Well the likely case of cheating would be Dom getting it on with another woman, but that's not what he's doing." Tabitha paused, and realized what she had said probably didn't make much sense at all to Rory.

"You lost me," he said, frowning, and as she assumed, he was confused.

"A new executive in his firm, a younger male, who is openly gay, has Dom feeling and doing things he's never done before."

"You can't be serious! The Dominic Tyler? I don't believe that for a second. Carrie has to be mistaken…" Rory was flabbergasted, and for a moment he actually managed to forget about his own craziness.

"As serious as a blowjob. Carrie saw them together. "

"Oh Jesus," Rory shook his head repeatedly, and closed his eyes, in an attempt to banish the image from his mind.

"Yeah, tell me about it. Carrie is sick over it."

"So Dom wants a divorce, too?"

"Oh no. He said it will never happen again. Apparently he can just shut those feelings off. He wants nothing to change. He went as far as to warn Carrie that she will lose everything, including the girls if she doesn't stay in their marriage."

"He's an asshole. She can take him for all he's got."

"That's what I told her. I helped her find a divorce lawyer. Tomorrow morning she has an appointment already." Rory nodded, and Tabitha had more on her mind. "Look, I said I was sorry earlier because I don't ever want you to feel like I am demeaning you. I appreciate you — and us — so much. We just need two incomes again. But our finances are nothing compared to the hell I'm watching Carrie go through. I'm just really happy you're mine, I know you love me as much as I love you, and together we've got this." *Of all times, of all things that Rory had just gotten messed up with. Forced into at the hand of Joe Morgan. He could hardly look at his wife.*

"Everything will be okay," he told her, but he was partly trying to convince himself of that fact as he held her in his arms again.

"Of course it will," she pulled back, and looked at him. *Really looked at him.* "Are you alright?"

"Yeah," he answered, attempting to sound convincing. But Tabitha was too perceptive for that. She knew him too well.

"Where were you just now?" she asked him.

"Out looking for a job, applying at places." Rory had only gone to one place, Donnewald, and he had not even made it inside.

"Any luck? I mean, did anyone say they are hiring now?"

"Not really," he answered.

"Did you make it to Donnewald?" Tabitha watched Rory nod his head and then look down at his feet on the floor.

"You're nervous, aren't you?" she asked, referring to having to put himself out there again in the working world, but Rory thought she had called him out as being on edge in front of her. As he most certainly was.

"No, Jesus. Just stop hounding me about a job. I will get one!" Rory lost his temper, and Tabitha immediately stepped into his space. The stress had gotten the best of him already.

"I don't want to fight about this," she told him, attempting to calm him, and she gently scratched her fingernails over the scruff on his face. There was something different about him still, and it was actually beginning to worry her.

"Me either," he told her, and then his cell phone buzzed in his pocket. Tabitha watched him reach for it and she leaned in to read the screen with him. They never had anything to hide from each other. And right now Rory had not immediately thought he needed to pull the phone back from her view. It was an unrecognizable number, but the text message was clearly for Rory.

Chance – pick up your first Yeti at 6 p.m. and deliver to the alley behind Gutch's.

They read it in unison. Actually, Tabitha had read it faster. She stepped back and looked at Rory. "What the hell? A Yeti? And since when are you delivering things in back alleys?"

Rory's eyes widened. He could lie to her, but he wasn't any good at thinking on his feet. He reached into his front pocket and pulled out the wad of cash. He threw it on the island's countertop near them. "I got a job today. Two thousand dollars up front. More cash will come tonight once I make that delivery."

"I don't understand," Tabitha said, attempting to count out the wad of bills on the countertop. "This is a ridiculous amount of money. Are you selling more of your things? This feels shady, but I know you. You're a good, honest man. Set me straight! Tell me you are not doing what this looks like you are doing!"

"If Joe Morgan has his way, by tonight, I'll officially be dealing for him."

The name of that man would forever take something from her each time she heard it. Tabitha instantly felt like she couldn't catch her breath. "He's a drug dealer? And you are messed up with him?" Tabitha's hands were trembling. The color drained from her face. Her world was spinning. She couldn't make sense of any of this.

"Calm down and listen to me," Rory helped her over to a stool near the island, and he sat down on the opposite one beside her. He pressed both of his knees to hers. "I am sick to my stomach over this, and now that I've gotten you involved, I swear to God, Tab, we have to be ready for that man to strike. He set me up. I drove into the lot at Donnewald to go in and apply for job. I was sitting in my truck and I witnessed Morgan dealing in broad daylight. He saw me. He assumed I was there looking for a job. The next thing I knew he was stuffing a wad of cash into my pocket, and he said he owned me. I don't know what to do. This is real trouble, Tab."

"You're going to the police, that's what you are going to do! Jesus, Rory. You cannot let that son of a bitch control you." Tabitha wanted to scream at him to *grow a pair of balls*, but he stopped her before she could. The fear on his face stripped her of her anger, and subsequently alarmed her. *This was about her. And his dire need to protect her.*

"He said he would hurt you. He brought up Beth, and then he said he would come after you. I can't. I won't let him. You are my whole world, the boys need you... I've already put you in such danger by telling you all of this."

Chapter Seventeen

On the exterior, Tabitha was a pillar of strength. Those closest to her, those she shared her innermost feelings with, knew however that she sometimes did things to humanize herself. There were fleeting honest glimpses of someone not so strong and confident. But most often, Tabitha Chance held everything together in her world. People perceived her as strong because she wanted them to.

When Tabitha and Rory walked out of the Hays Police Department on Twelfth Street, she slowly took in the fresh air through her nostrils. The wind, for a moment, consumed her airways, and she was relieved to be outside. It was stuffy inside of that building. Her hands had been clammy for the past hour. Rory had not committed a crime. He was free to go wherever he chose, but at six o'clock that evening, he was instructed by the police to follow Joe Morgan's orders to retrieve the Yeti and deliver it to the alley behind Gutch's Bar and Grill. There would be a police tail on him, in an effort to catch Joe Morgan — or anyone involved in peddling opioids with him.

Once they were back inside of Rory's truck, he spoke. "I know I did the right thing by telling you and going to the police, but to Joe Morgan it's going to be a stupid move. He thought he had me, and when he finds out I've defied him, he will be livid. I swear I am not going to let you out of my sight until he's behind bars."

Tabitha squeezed his knee as she sat in the passenger seat beside him. She wasn't the kind of woman to cling, to fall apart. But she was terrified knowing what he had walked into. *Wrong place. At the absolute worst time.* "I know he's dangerous, especially now that we've discovered this about him." Tabitha contemplated in the past few hours *if Beth had known?* She chose to believe not. Beth never would have stayed with him. She would not have accepted a criminal into her life. "Joe Morgan is the type of person who pushes and shoves until he is one rung on the ladder above everyone else. He was that way with Beth…" Tabitha paused. The fact that she was gone, and only a memory, would always deeply pain her. "And now he's trying to manipulate you. This isn't over, Rory. A lot can go wrong, even when you think the police have your back."

Carrie couldn't paint. Her focus was elsewhere, so she went home to a big, empty house. Her thoughts were consumed with Dom and how everything in their life together was about to be drastically altered. The twins needed to be told. Carrie wondered how they would react. *Had they sensed the distance between their parents? Would they hold them at fault for not trying harder? Would they blame one over the other for love lost, a family severed?* So much of their world was going to be divided among them. His and hers would now have to be yours or mine.

She sat on a high-back, cushioned chair at the long, rectangular kitchen table for eight. The color of the chairs was ivory, a rich-looking shade of off-white with barely a tint of yellow. That house had the grandest and best of everything in it, but right now she couldn't remember a time when any of that really mattered to her. She was happiest when she had Dom's love and attention, when their girls were small and life was pleasantly chaotic. Money and power had changed Dom. He wanted things she didn't understand. *Especially now.*

Carrie was so lost in thought that she had not heard Dom walk in. Clad in a black suit with a paisley gray tie, and his classic flat-soled tie dress shoes were back on his feet. She knew exactly why he no longer wore the loafers. "I stopped by the gallery, and Sharon told me you were here." Carrie assumed he was on his lunch break, but she never asked. She couldn't remember the last time he *stopped by the gallery,* and she hadn't brought that up to him either. "I have an hour before my next meeting. I thought we could talk." He sat down on the chair directly across the table from her.

She wanted to ask him if he would like something to eat, or drink. But then, she reminded herself that he was about to no longer be hers to take care of anymore. So again, she stayed silent.

"Your silence always did bother me. I would rather have you yell and scream, just be angry, than not speak to me at all."

Carrie looked at her husband, long and hard. "I am angry," she finally said. "I'm mad as hell at you because you broke us."

Dom nodded. He never looked away from her this time. It was as if he was past the shame. "But broken can be fixed."

"Not all things," she added with a certainty that worried him.

"I disagree," he told her. "I messed up, but I'm going to fix this. We love each other. We have the girls to think about, to keep us all together as a family."

"Funny, I don't know the last time we told each other, 'I love you.'" Carrie was to blame for that, too, as she had noted. She didn't address what he said about the girls. She couldn't. Because it pained her too much. She dreaded telling them of the divorce. She wouldn't bad mouth their father. Not ever. She promised herself that. But perhaps one day they would learn the truth.

"I know how hurt you are," Dom began again.

"Do you?" Carrie immediately interjected. "Did you witness me getting intimate with another person?" She chose her words with caution and was careful to say person. She was not a critical woman. She didn't judge. She accepted different people in this world. She just never thought her husband would be one of them.

"I was caught up in something stupid. I regret it like you wouldn't believe. Please, Carrie. Please forgive me."

In time, Carrie hoped with all of her heart that she could forgive her husband. But forgetting would never happen. Not in her lifetime. Not after this kind of hurt. "I have an appointment with an attorney tomorrow morning. I want a divorce." Carrie, always honest and upfront, wondered if she should have taken Tabitha's advice and not told Dom that detail until after she had a plan in place with the divorce lawyer.

"That's a mistake, you know it is," Dom's face flushed to the roots of his short cropped gray hair all over his head. "Think about the girls!"

"I have, and I am," Carrie replied. "I want them to grow to be women who respect others, and themselves. No woman should stay with a man who is unfaithful. They may be too young to realize that now, but they will in time. To stay with you would not be who I am. I don't want to live wondering if another late night meeting means you're dropping your pants for someone else. I don't want to wonder if you're coming home to me, and giving me some type of sexually transmitted disease because you have not been true to me, and only me, as I have to you. Always. I don't want to live that kind of life. I don't want you anymore." Carrie had no idea where the strength within her suddenly stemmed from. She was only certain that she had to say this before she lost her courage and completely fell apart. Because unraveling was all she really felt like doing at this awful transitional moment in their lives. Their marriage was over, because Carrie didn't want to save it. That was a fact. But truly, Dom was the one who wrecked their life together.

"You're not going to go through with this," he told her. "You need time to process before you act on impulse and run to a lawyer to plot your best settlement. I've already told you. This house is mine, and the girls will stay with me."

"When you speak to me like that, that is the reason I need a lawyer. You cannot threaten me. I have a right to half of all of this, and our girls will be shared between us, too."

"I'm not threatening you, Carrie. I'm just telling you how it is. If you leave me, you leave all of this behind — including Sheridan and Jess."

He could have the mansion on the hill, and its entirety, but the thought of losing her girls terrified her. "I'm not some sort of business deal that you can come out ahead with. I am your wife."

"Let's hope you choose to keep it that way. You *are* my wife."

The man across the table was barely recognizable to her sometimes. This was one of those moments. "I will not be for long, because I *choose* to divorce you!"

"What?" Carrie and Dom both looked up in unison. That house was too big to hear if anyone was coming or going. In the doorway, which led out of the kitchen and into the living room, stood her girls. Side by side and wide-eyed. Jess had been the one to speak in astonishment. And Sheridan looked equally as shocked.

"Girls!" Carrie said. "What you are doing home already?" School dismissal was not for another two and a half hours.

"It's a half day, and you obviously forgot," Jess spoke again.

"Tori's mom brought us home after she saw us waiting around forever for you," Sheridan added, "and you weren't answering your cell phone."

"Oh my goodness, I am so sorry! That completely slipped my mind." Carrie was instantly disappointed in herself for letting them down. She always had their schedule together. Everything was posted on the kitchen wall calendar, and etched in her mind. She was not one of those mothers who didn't have her life, and their schedules, together.

Jess shrugged, and Sheridan added, "It's fine, mom."

"Girls, come sit down," Carrie told them, and Dom shook his head at her. The girls both saw his disapproval. They obeyed her request, and joined their parents at the kitchen table.

"Is everything alright?" Jess spoke first. "We both heard what you said, mom. A divorce? You and dad are splitting up? We are going to be a broken family!"

Carrie watched Dom reach for his dramatic daughter. Jess was seated in the chair right next to his, and he wrapped his big, strong arm around her. "Your mother is not happy here anymore," Dom bluntly told their daughters.

"That's not true!" Carrie protested in her own defense. No one else was going to stand up for her, and the lie her children's father had just told them. "Your dad and I have grown apart. When couples start to hurt each other in ways that cannot be repaired, it's time to separate and mend apart."

"So you are just going to take some time apart, like a mutual separation, and then you will get back together?" Sheridan's words were so hopeful that they made Carrie wish that were true. She was seated in the chair right next to Carrie. And Carrie reached for her hand as she spoke.

"No, honey," Carrie told her. "It's going to be permanent. Your dad and I are getting a divorce." Both of the girls cried. Jess was in Dom's arms, and Sheridan found comfort in her mother's embrace. Carrie tried her damndest not to fall apart and cry with them.

"Why!" Jess demanded to know. Through her hysterical tears, she looked up at her father for answers. Carrie glared at Dom. Their daughters were counting on him. She, one last time, was depending on her husband to honor her and respect her decision. They were parents first now. They had no marriage left to nurture.

"Because your mother wants this, that's why," Dom spoke, not like a father, but like a businessman, sealing the deal to make himself come out looking so flawless that he shined.

"I don't want to leave this house, or live anywhere else!" Jess protested again, as Sheridan stayed silent.

"I agree, baby girl," Dom told her, still holding her close to him with one of his giant arms wrapped around her slim eleven-year-old body. "This house will always be ours."

"I'm living here with Dad!" Jess blurted out as if she never gave her mother — and all the love and nurturing and absolutely everything she had ever done for her — a second thought. "Sherdian, you're staying too, right?" Carrie felt the blood drain from her face when she turned to look at her daughter beside her. Sheridan was the good, faithful and trustworthy child that she could always count on. The very last thing Carrie would ever want to do would be to split up her girls. They were twins. Bonded closely, and forever connected. But the thought of Sheridan siding with Jess and Dom had begun to suck the life out of Carrie. She didn't have to hear Sheridan's answer. The look in her eyes already gave her away. *She was most faithful to her twin sister.*

"We are getting ahead of ourselves here!" Carrie demanded their attention with her panicked tone. She watched Dom send her a look of *I told you so.* And she cringed. "Girls, go up to your rooms or find something to do elsewhere. Just leave this kitchen. Your father and I have to finish this discussion, alone." Carrie continued to appear to be the bad guy, as Dom sat innocently in the presence of his daughters who both absolutely adored him. They both left the kitchen crying. It broke Carrie's heart to watch them cling to each other.

When she knew for certain that they were out of earshot, Carrie spoke with adamancy, but she kept her voice low. "How dare you make this look like it's all me!"

"Is it a lie that you are not happy here anymore?" Dom asked her outright.

"You and I have not been happy together for a very long time. That's the truth. But, what is the underlying cause to that truth? It takes two people to keep the love and the passion alive in a marriage. You may claim to still love me, but your passion was elsewhere. Clearly, I cannot tell our daughters that!"

Dom cringed. He knew she would never. His wife was not that kind of woman, or mother. He trusted her with his darkest secret. But the mere thought of his girls knowing what he was capable of doing just to peak his curiosity and indulge in fleeting pleasure, nearly sickened him.

"I am ashamed of what I did," he admitted. "It would destroy me if they knew." Dom suddenly turned vulnerable, and Carrie was unnerved. This was not fair to her at all.

"And you don't think that it's killing me to know you could take my daughters away from me?"

"I'm glad you're finally starting to see my side of things. I *will* take them away from you. It's not a matter of I can, or I might. I most certainly will."

Carrie broke down and cried at the table, right in front of her husband. He never reached for her. He only stared. She was at a loss. She felt trapped at his hand. He saw this as her moment of defeat. "Call off your lawyer and this preposterous idea of leaving me and our family."

She shook her head no.

"Then be prepared to lose everything," Dom stated coldly, before he got up from the table and walked away from her. Carrie didn't feel like his wife anymore. She felt like part of a business deal. One of which she was on the losing end.

Chapter Eighteen

It was six o'clock p.m. Dom never came home for dinner, and Carrie had offered to order pizza for the twins, but neither one of them claimed to be hungry. When both Jess and Sheridan weren't giving Carrie their silence, they were begging her not to divorce their father. Jess especially was adamant about her mother keeping their family together. Carrie wanted to tell her daughters that their father did something that she cannot forgive him for, but she held back. The truth would only make this matter worse. Instead, she closed herself in her bedroom and sat between the ivory cushions on her sofa. She would miss retreating to that corner of the house. That sofa had been her safe place when she needed to think, or cry, through the years. She held her cell phone in her hand and tried to call Tabitha. That call immediately went to voicemail.

Tabitha was told to stay home. Rory thought he had convinced her to do as he asked, to keep herself and their boys safe. Tabitha was certain the boys would be fine, downstairs in the basement playing video games, when she told them she had a quick errand to run. They asked if their dad was home, she told them no, but he would be back soon, too.

The original text from Joe Morgan had instructed Rory to pick up a Yeti at six, and deliver it to the alley behind Gutch's Bar and Grill. Rory had no information on the location for the pickup. He knew that was Joe Morgan's way of forcing him to respond to his text, and *RSVP* to his dirty work. He wanted to know for certain that Rory had not backed down. The police told Rory how to respond to the text when he and Tabitha were at the station. Rory had replied, *Place for pickup?* And Joe Morgan's response was *Mailbox 501 on South Clinton.* Rory concluded, with the police, that Joe Morgan was being cautious and wanted to remain unseen. There would be no direct hand-off between Joe Morgan and Rory. The Yeti, however, would have to be hand-delivered to someone in the back alley of Gutch's, and the police wanted that person. Rory's job tonight was to lead them to the criminal. The person, presumably who wanted the drugs, would give Rory another wad of cash in exchange for the opioid-filled Yeti. It was a clever scheme, which most likely had been ongoing for some time, but the police would raid it tonight. With Rory's help.

He was nervous as he drove his truck slowly down South Clinton Street, looking from side to side for the number 501 to be posted on one of those mailboxes. And then, to his immediate right, he found it. Rory applied the brakes on his truck, and shifted the gear into park on the side of the road next to that ordinary black mailbox with the white adhesive-backed numbers stuck to it. He was told not to look around, just to get out of his truck at a normal pace, retrieve the Yeti, and get back inside.

Two blocks back, Tabitha sat curbside behind the steering wheel of her car, with her headlights now off, and the engine still running. She followed him. She knew the police had to be close by somewhere, staked out and also watching Rory, but she had not been able to spot them. Tabitha assumed she had already been seen by them, but she didn't care. She was there for Rory. There was no way she could sit idle at home while her husband was taking part in something ridiculously dangerous. Tabitha could have thrown up as her nerves were getting the best of her right now. She saw the screen on her muted phone light up when Carrie's call came through. She declined it and sent it directly to voicemail. *Not now, Care, she thought to herself, but just wait until I tell you about this later.* Tabitha hoped to God she would have a positive ending to share after this craziness. She still worried that Rory was going to be held criminally responsible for something in this mess created by Joe Morgan.

Despite the fact that Rory thought he would go into cardiac arrest from the way his pulse took off inside his chest, he retrieved the Yeti from the mailbox and made his way back inside of his truck without incident. That was the easy part, he assumed now, as he turned his truck around in the middle of the vacant road. His next stop would be the alley behind Gutch's. And God only knew who he was going to find waiting for him there.

Tabitha fretted about where to go. She didn't want to be too close to the exchange taking place in the alley, so she parked her car in the crowded lot facing the bar and grill. She turned off the engine and kept her doors locked. She sat there in her dark car not knowing what to do. She had been ahead of Rory en route there, and when she saw truck lights coming down the alley, Tabitha got out of her car and made her way far across the parking lot where she squatted down between two other parked cars to be in direct, but still far enough away, view of the alley. She watched Rory turn off the headlights on his truck. What Tabitha couldn't see was the person walking behind Rory's truck and alongside of the bed of it before she stood directly in front of Rory's driver's side window. Rory rolled down his window. The Yeti was placed between his legs on the seat. Strangely, he immediately relaxed when he saw that the person standing alongside of his truck was a woman. She was wearing too high of heels with a short skirt and her blonde hair was styled as if she was making a comeback with big hair from the 80s. She reeked of too much perfume. "The Yeti," she told Rory, and he watched her painted red lips move. Some of that over-applied lipstick had smudged onto a front tooth of hers. Rory reached for the cup between his legs. As he held it up, he watched the woman pull out a wad of cash from in between her breasts. It was like a bad scene from a movie he never wanted to watch again. Once Rory had the money in his hand, and the Yeti was in hers, there were bright lights from both directions. In front of them and behind them. The alley was then blocked off, on both ends, by police cars with blaring sirens and flashing lights. Within the beams of those direct, blinding lights, Rory watched at least a half a dozen uniformed police officers charge the scene on foot. Guns were drawn.

Voices were raised. *Put your hands up. Hays PD. You are under arrest.*

Rory sat inside of his truck and did nothing more. He only hoped that his part in this mess, concocted by Joe Morgan, was over.

But it wasn't.

Joe Morgan had the same idea as Tabitha. *Be there, but be out of sight. Mesh with the crowded parking lot full of cars, but still be a witness to what had gone down in the alley.*

One of the vehicles that Tabitha had crouched down beside was not vacant. And Tabitha shockingly became aware of that once the police were preoccupied with the arrest. The alley was bustling. The attention was on the criminal and perhaps Rory, the man who aided a drug bust tonight. Tabitha considered this to be a good time to escape to her car and drive back home. Her husband would be home, safe and sound, soon. But when she got up to her feet again, she heard his unmistakable voice. "Looks like we're on the same wavelength tonight." Tabitha's eyes widened. *She had to be ready to run. If he tried to pull her into his vehicle, she was prepared to scream at the top of her lungs. If he did succeed at dragging her into his truck, she would throw herself out of it once they started moving. A broken limb would be worth her escape from the danger of that man.* Tabitha stared up and at Joe Morgan sitting in the driver's seat of his black Silverado. "Your husband made the wrong move tonight. My girl, Melodi, is being cuffed and questioned in that alley right now. She knows better than to rat me out. Your husband, however, did not."

"That's because Rory is not like you," Tabitha defended him. "He's good and honest."

"And stupid. Don't forget stupid. I told him what the repercussions would be if he crossed me. You, my love, are the price he will pay." Joe Morgan's words, *my love,* ricocheted through her body, as Tabitha abruptly backed farther away from the truck, and him. She bumped her lower back into another car's side mirror, which slowed her for a moment.

"Go ahead, run. This isn't the time or place for me to act. Just watch yourself. Be alert. Because I will be back." It was a blur to Tabitha how quickly she was able to make her way back to her car. But there was no confusion regarding Joe Morgan's words to her. *He would come after her.* She wanted to make her way to the police right then and there, but Joe Morgan had already nonchalantly drove out of the parking lot and away from the scene of the crime which he initiated in that dark alley.

Chapter Nineteen

The first thing that Tabitha did when she walked in the door at home was she locked it behind her. And secondly, she poured herself a full glass of wine. Her hands trembled as she sat down at the kitchen island and took her first, long sip. She could hear the boys carrying on as they were still playing video games downstairs. That was best, because she didn't need Dane's perceptive nature right now. He would know something was wrong with her. He was her sensitive son, and would make a wonderful husband one day. Tabitha was certain of it.

She tried to call Rory as she sat there. *He should be coming home soon.* But, he never picked up. Then, she called Carrie.

Carrie answered on the second ring. "Hey, thanks for calling me back." Tabitha had forgotten that she let a call from Carrie go to her voicemail when she was sitting in her dark car on South Clinton Street, watching Rory retrieve an illegal drug-filled Yeti from a stranger's mailbox. *What a night.*

"You okay?" Tabitha asked her before taking another drink of her wine.

"Not really. It's Dom. My life is falling to pieces. Can you meet me at the gallery to talk for awhile?" Neither one of them liked lengthy phone conversations and had always been partial to in-person meetings. Beth used to chide them both about that. She enjoyed having a phone pressed to her ear.

"I really can't leave here tonight," Tabitha spoke, and realized how vague she had sounded. "I have something to tell you though, too. It's important. Can you come over? Rory is out and I'm here with the boys, but they're consumed with video games in the dungeon," *as they called it.*

"I'll leave my house in a few minutes." Carrie hung up the phone and sighed. At least someone was still a constant in her life. *Dom had failed her, and the girls had chosen him.*

Tabitha opened the door before Carrie made her way to it from the sidewalk outside. One look at her and Carrie knew something was wrong. When Carrie followed her into the house, Tabitha already had a glass of wine poured for her.

"Thank you. I need this so badly," Carrie took a long drink, "but, you go first. Tell me what's going on. I haven't seen you look this upset since — " Carrie stopped. She didn't need to bring up that awful night again. Minus the sheer panic of that night, however, Tabitha did look almost as rattled.

"You are not going to believe this. After I left you this afternoon, I came home and Rory was out. He went looking for a job. He ended up at Donnewald because his friend Ryker who works there said they were hiring. Well, Rory ended up witnessing a drug deal in the parking lot. Joe Morgan was the dealer."

"For the love of God, he's even worse than we thought!" Carrie interrupted, and Tabitha nodded along and continued.

"Rory was seen. Joe Morgan basically threatened him. He shoved a large sum of cash at him, told him he owned him now. He hooked him up with a drug deal going down tonight, and told him if he didn't deliver, that he would come after me."

"Oh my God! What are you even saying? This is unreal. Hasn't that man already caused enough destruction in our lives? You called the police, right?"

"Yes, I forced Rory after he finally told me. Jesus, I know him and I could see that something was consuming him. He was trying to protect me, but I swear I could have beaten the shit out of him for considering doing the deal."

Tabitha proceeded to tell Carrie that the police used Rory to botch the drug deal in the alley behind Gutch's tonight. She admitted that she followed him, and then she filled her in on the worst part. Joe Morgan being in the parking lot.

"You are not safe!" Carrie flipped out. "I recently had a run-in with him outside of my gallery. I intended to tell you about it. We just exchanged a few words, basically me telling him to keep walking, before I sped off. It's like he's stalking us, you more than me obviously."

"I haven't even told Rory what happened yet. He thinks I've been home all night."

"Where is he anyway?"

"Still with the police, I assume."

"I'm not leaving you here alone until he gets here," Carrie stated adamantly.

"I'm not alone. The boys are here. But yeah, stay with me." Tabitha reached for Carrie's hand and held it. "Keep my mind off of this crazy, and tell me why you initially called me. How bad are things at your house?"

Carrie felt her eyes get teary. "Bad. Dom pleaded with me to carry on with our marriage and our life as a family. He wants to me to believe nothing will ever happen again, and that he'll stay faithful. I can't. I just can't get that sickening image out of my head. I won't go back to him. But there are consequences if I don't. He basically will kick me out. He'll keep the house — and our girls will live with him. He said it doesn't matter if I hire a lawyer to fight him, because he will win. And the saddest part of all of this is my girls have sided with him." Carrie choked on a sob.

"What? They know?"

"They came home early from school. I forgot to pick them up. They walked in on Dom and I talking about getting a divorce. I said I wanted one. Dom told the girls that I am no longer happy living there. I couldn't tell them why. I can't tarnish their father in their young, innocent eyes. They adore him."

"Well you can't give them the details of what you saw, but you can tell them that he was unfaithful!" Tabitha wanted to put a foot up her best friend's ass. She always played the good, righteous hand and sometimes it left her used and abused. But, this time, it was going to cost her dearly.

"Well I haven't, and Jess was unwavering about staying with Dom. Sheridan, I think, was torn, but you know how she assumed the role of her sister's protector for basically all of their lives. I can't separate them. They need each other."

"And you need to be with your children!" Tabitha was angry. "You better be planning to keep that appointment with the attorney tomorrow. Someone needs to get through to you. You can win. You are their mother. Dom has rights, sure, but no judge will take your girls away from you."

"I desperately needed to hear that," Carrie spoke before she finished off the wine in her glass. Then Tabitha got up to pour more for each of them.

Before they could resume their conversation, Rory finally walked in the front door. Tabitha met him in the middle of the kitchen and held onto him for a moment. She was beyond relieved to have him home, safe and unharmed. When they separated, Rory looked cautiously at both Tabitha and Carrie before he spoke.

"It's okay, she knows," Tabitha told him.

"I could hug you, too," Carrie stated. "Thank God you got yourself out of that mess." But it wasn't over.

"The police arrested a woman, she said she was the dealer's lover, but she would not name Morgan. She's in custody downtown. I was free to go after some more questioning. Morgan is still out there, getting by with this. I sure as hell hope that he screws up somewhere along the line so they can catch him and put him away for the rest of his life. I actually felt sorry for the woman. She was really shaken up. It was almost as if tonight was her first time taking part in a deal. She looked as nervous as I felt."

"So what happens next? What did the police tell you to do?" Tabitha asked him.

"To keep my eyes open, watch my back. And to report anything else that comes up with Joe Morgan. Otherwise, we go on living." Rory seemed less tense, which made Tabitha contemplate telling him the rest of her story.

"Tell him, Tab…" It was just like Carrie to morph into Mother Teresa. Tabitha shot her a look.

"You're one to talk about telling the whole story!" Tabitha snapped at her, but winked afterward. My goodness those two loved each other. It was as if they were made from the same colliding cluster of stars. There were shared, equal parts of them that pulled them toward each other like gravity. Beth was a part of that indefinable magic as well. And now that she was gone, it was as if Tabitha and Carrie were even stronger. Beth perhaps had left that gift behind for them. A part of her soul would always be with the two of them. That, they were certain of.

"Tell me what?" Rory was the one who shot a look this time. At Tabitha.

"I left tonight. I followed you to South Clinton… and then I parked in Gutch's lot."

"You did what? Jesus, Tabitha! You could have been killed. I had no idea what I was walking into!"

"Exactly. That's why I couldn't just sit here and wait like a good wife. That's never been me, and you married the wrong bitch if you think I'll ever shut up and listen." Carrie giggled and Rory shook his head at his wife.

"So what happened? Did you just leave after the police arrived?"

"Well that was my intention. I was crouched down between parked cars. I thought I was the only one out there, but turns out I was wrong." Rory's eyes widened. He already knew what she would say next. And panic ensued him at the mere thought of Joe Morgan being anywhere near his wife. Tabitha knew that Rory realized Joe Morgan had been there, too, so she told him the truth. "He was not happy that you disobeyed his orders and went to the police."

"What else did he say? Did he touch you at all?" Rory felt his blood pressure rise. A heaviness rose to his chest.

"No, no. I stayed back from him. I was prepared to run, and I did get away safely."

"But not before he had something to say to you, right? Tab, tell me. Now."

"He told me to go. He said it wasn't the time or place for him to act. He said for me to be alert, because he would be back."

"No!" Rory ran his fingers through his thick brown hair, and momentarily covered his face with the open palms of both of his hands. He looked like he needed sleep, but the worry and panic in him would likely not allow his mind to rest. "The police must be aware of this. And you need twenty-four hour protection. I want an officer outside of this house — or at the hospital! Wherever you are, you need to be kept safe from him." Carrie sat there watching them, and hearing them. She was in awe of how Rory spoke to Tabitha. Oddly now, she felt pangs of envy. He loved her unconditionally. He would die before he saw her hurt. It was storybook for a man to love a woman like that, and Carrie wholeheartedly wished she and Dom had been able to be more of the same, and could have had their happily ever after, instead of a heartbreakingly sudden ending.

Chapter Twenty

The Hays Police Department lacked the manpower to give up an officer to pose as a personal security guard for Tabitha. Rory's request was basically unheard of to them anyway, but they assured him of the standard patrolled drive-bys of their neighborhood and house. They were watching Joe Morgan closely. *He wouldn't have a prayer if he screwed up.* Even still, Rory was on edge when Tabitha left alone the following morning for another twelve-hour shift at the hospital.

Carrie walked into the gallery. Sharon had the morning off, so it had been closed for the few hours that Carrie was also gone. She just returned from her attorney's office. She hired the divorce attorney after a two-hour-long consultation, but not without reservations. Kristie Weh was one of the fiercest lawyers Hays had ever encountered in the courtroom. She had gotten many women through divorce, child custody and visitation, and alimony. Even still, Carrie was torn. When she shared her story, she again left out the details of Dom's affair. The fact that she caught him with another man wasn't pertinent, she thought, because it felt as if she was stooping low, and playing dirty. That was not who Carrie was. She was respectable and honorable, but the sad truth was Dom had played on those characteristics of hers and was counting on her vulnerability. He expected her to cave. The fact that Carrie had gone as far as to hire an attorney was going to be an eye-opener to him. For most of their marriage, Dom had his wife where he wanted her. She raised their girls. She had a serious hobby that turned into a career that fulfilled her. But she was always at the helm of their family. Dom provided well financially for all of them, and Carrie handled everything else. He had taken her for granted. And now he would realize he also underestimated her.

She turned the OPEN sign in the front window after she flipped on the lights in the gallery. No matter how much scented fragrance wax she burned daily, for hours on end, it always initially smelled musty when she walked into that old building. Nevertheless Carrie loved that place and everything about it. The building alone had an artsy, vintage feel to it. She never tired of spending her days in that atmosphere, surrounded by her very own artwork displayed in the gallery, and among her unfinished inspiration in the back studio. She felt a sense of accomplishment there. And today, she hung onto that feeling more than ever — because her world at home was unrecognizable now. And that was about to get worse with the changes ahead.

Dom had left for work early. They slept apart again and mostly shared silence unless the girls were around and they had attempted to force as much small talk as they could stand. Dom seemed to try harder at it than Carrie. When she drove the girls to school, the mood in the car was somber. No one wanted to bring up how their family was dangling by a measly thread. But the girls, both of them, had made Carrie feel as if she had the power to save their family. Even still, she kept her appointment to consult with a lawyer, and then made the decision to file for divorce from her husband. One day, her daughters would understand. She hoped.

Carrie was lost in thought, feeling sulky and miserable, when the chime on the storefront's door rang. *She had a customer.*

She turned to greet whoever had come in to browse, or perhaps pick up a preorder. And that's when she saw him. Standing a few steps in from the doorway, Joe Morgan wore his beer distributing uniform. Grayish-blue pants, and a matching pinstriped shirt with a deep pocket over the left breast. He had something bulky, possibly a cell phone, in it and it was weighting down the thin material of the shirt. His hair was jet-black and overly jelled with product. His face was attractive, but given who that man was and all that Carrie had known, that face was one to loath. And now fear.

Carrie stood silent and stared, forcing *her customer* to speak first. "Good morning," Joe Morgan said to her. "It's a windy one out there."

"It's always windy in Hays," she responded, trying to buy herself a little time to think. *What did he want from her? And how would she protect herself if she gravely needed to?* Behind the counter was an empty wooden container with a flip lid. It was heavy and sturdy, and it had the shape of an old cigar box. An order of paintbrushes years back had been shipped in it. The paintbrushes were long used, and now only she and Sharon had known what was kept in that empty box. A concealed carry pistol that Carrie declined to keep on her body or in her handbag, but she wanted it for protection there in the gallery if either of them had ever been prompted to defend themselves in a dire situation. Both women were inexperienced with guns, but they had taken the concealed carry class to gain the necessary knowledge. At least they were aware of how to point and shoot the hidden, loaded gun. Carrie pushed that thought from her mind. This didn't have to turn crazy. He just needed to leave.

"I had a delivery down the street," he began, maybe to explain why he was there. Carrie continued to listen, but found it very difficult to ignore the panic rising in her chest. "While in your neighborhood, I thought I would stop in. I've never been inside of here before."

"Can I help you with something, or did you just want to look around?" Carrie only wanted him to leave. Her face remained stoic, and she had hoped he could not read the uneasiness she harbored.

"I can browse while we talk," he stated, and Carrie did not respond to him. She had absolutely no desire to speak or listen to him. A part of her wished another customer would walk in to botch his quest to be there — and to talk to her. "I doubt that you are clueless about what went down last night. You girls are tight. One can't make a move without sharing every little detail with the other. I know, I remember Beth's constant tales about the three of you. She talked about you so damn much that I felt like I knew you both exceptionally well." The mention of Beth from his lips and the references he made of their friendship had shaken her. He was the reason she was gone. Regardless of whose hands held that dagger, Joe Morgan was to blame. There was no uncertainty about that in Carrie's mind. "Anyway, the police are watching me. There's probably an unmarked car across the street right now. I don't know, and really I don't care. Eventually, they will lose interest in me."

"What are you doing here?" Carrie interrupted him. "Just put it out there. Why are you here?"

"Impatience is unattractive on a woman," he rudely stated, and she only stared. "Why am I here? Perhaps because you're an easier target that Tabitha right now. And I actually think that you can give me what I need, just as well as she can." Carrie flinched. And he noticed. "You don't have to be afraid of me." She wasn't successfully pulling off pretending to keep her calm around him.

"I'm not afraid, just uncomfortable," Carrie spoke honestly, and she didn't chide herself for the admission. "The sight of you upsets me, and for good reason."

"Beth... yes, I understand," he paused. "It's always going to come back to Beth for us, isn't it? What she did left us reeling. She took her own life. And what a way to go..." Joe Morgan had shifted to speaking in a callous, heartless tone, and Carrie was sickened a million times over by him now. "You know, the last exchange she and I had, was not good. Relationships fail. They end. It took a long time for that to sink in to Beth's mind, or her heart. She loved passionately that's for sure." Carrie wanted to shut this man up. She wanted to see him suffer dearly for all of the pain, confusion, and the devastation that he caused Beth. "I should have been taken aback by what she did, or more clearly, how she did it. But I was not. I've never shared this with anyone before, but it's probably time that I did. I guess, just like everyone else, I'm looking for peace from this, too." Carrie didn't believe him. He was immoral. He didn't need peace.

He kept talking. "I was taking a shower in the privacy of my own home that night when Beth waltzed in as if she owned the place, or me. I was not hers to claim or to keep. I was tired of her. Plain and simple. I wanted her gone and she was like a bad rash that kept on resurfacing." Carrie had tears in her eyes now. The ill speak of her dearest friend gone too soon pained her beyond belief. Joe Morgan immediately noticed that he had gotten to her. And that empowered him to continue on.

"I said and did absolutely everything to break her of me, and I told her precisely that. Everything except for putting a knife through her heart."

Carrie stumbled back two steps. She couldn't catch her breath. In Beth's absolute weakest state of mind, Joe Morgan had put that unthinkable, horrific idea into her head. She could have thrown up right then and there at her own feet. This man and all that he miserably stood for repulsed her beyond comprehension.

She was completely overwhelmed and could barely handle what he was telling her, but she managed to speak. "So you do see it? It's your fault that she's dead." The word *dead* riveted through her. It was too final. Too absolute. "She was so consumed with you that she did as you told her. Or maybe, to spite you. Maybe she wanted you to be haunted by it."

He laughed, mocking her suggestion. "Haunted, huh? I don't believe in that bullshit. What's gone is gone. Nothing ricochets back."

"That's where you're wrong. Karma comes flying back when you least expect it. You will get yours, you son of a bitch!" Carrie spat those words at him, fueled by all of her hatred for him. Yes, she feared him, but her anger suddenly overpowered her fear.

"That's what they say…" he halfheartedly agreed.

"Just get out of here!" Carrie escalated her voice at him again.

He turned, and it appeared that he was going to leave. He took a few steps toward the door before he stopped and spoke again. "Beth wanted kids of her own. She was so taken by other people's children, and obsessed with the fact that everyone else had what she didn't." He paused. "Jess is her name right?"

Carrie's eyes widened. "One of your daughters? Jess was Beth's godchild, right? Pretty girl. Defiant too, from what I remember." Fearing this man for herself, and for Tabitha, was one thing, but when Joe Morgan spoke her daughter's name and almost boasted of knowing something about her, that was altogether different. At this moment, Carrie completely understood how and why Beth had lost her mind over Joe Morgan. He was an evil person. A master manipulator. *What did he want from them, any of them?* Beth was gone and he was suddenly entirely too present in their lives.

"I don't know what you want from any of us," Carrie spoke through clenched teeth, "but I do know that you're done hurting the people I love. I will tear you apart with my bare hands if you ever go near either one of my children." Carrie didn't recognize the person she was right now, and most certainly had been taken aback by her own spoken words. She avoided confrontation. She was all about keeping the peace. But she was a mother and this man had indirectly threatened her daughter. He showed an interest in her, and Carrie had come undone.

"And here I thought you were the good girl with the nice persona radiating from that chubby frame," he chuckled, again disrespecting and mocking her. "Hays Middle School, right? That's the school she attends?" Joe Morgan was egging her on. Forcing her hand. Carrie was overcome with desperation. She imagined the worst. *Jess. Her little girl.* He was a drug dealer. A dangerous, harmful man in who knows how many other ways. She walked past the cash register and stood behind the counter. He thought she was just putting distance between them.

"I have work to do. I want you out of here, or I will call the police." She stood directly in front of the wooden box. Both of her arms hung straight down at her sides. She could easily reach and flip the unlatched lid.

"And what would you tell them? I came in here as a customer," he defended himself. "Do I scare you, Carrie? Does the thought of me befriending your child rattle you? If it doesn't, it should." The moment he spoke those words, he turned his back to Carrie as if he was going to leave that threat hanging for her to lose her mind over. But what he didn't know was she was already unraveling. The depth of her grief for Beth was resurfacing. Whenever she was around Joe Morgan, it worsened. And now her marriage was over. Her husband had hurt her in the most horrible way. She was embarrassed and mortified. All of her emotions were spiraling. Carrie simply reacted.

She grabbed for her gun. She aimed it at him. It all happened so fast. She spun out of control. His back was to her. He was oblivious to how far he had actually pushed her. Shoved her. All that solely circled through her mind was that if he got away, he would hurt Jess. She pulled the trigger and the weapon fired. Carrie never hesitated as Joe Morgan instantly spun around the second he heard and saw what was happening. And it all went down in a split second. The bullet that would have gone into his back now felt as if it shattered his shoulder and there was instant blood pooling underneath and through the short sleeved shirt of his uniform. Joe grabbed for his shoulder, clenching it hard, as blood seeped through his fingers. Panic ensued for the both of them. "You bitch!" he yelled at her. She had a bad aim. It wasn't the best possible shot she could have taken. At least not if she wanted him dead. But she didn't. She just wanted him gone. And now, the very last thing she was going to let him do was bleed to death on the floor of her gallery. Carrie reached for her phone and frantically called 911, as reality sunk in fast that she would have some serious repercussions to deal with.

Chapter Twenty-one

Hays police officer arrived at the gallery first. It was possible that he had already been in the vicinity after he had followed Joe Morgan downtown, just to keep a close watch. Not close enough though as Joe Morgan had spent too much time making threats before he drove Carrie to do the unthinkable. *She shot him.* Carrie never moved from standing behind the counter. But, clenching his wounded arm, he made his way toward her. "I need something to apply pressure to this!" He sounded alarmed, but strangely in control. Carrie grabbed for a folded towel underneath the counter. As she gave it to him, law enforcement arrived. *She broke the law.*

The middle-aged male in uniform rushed to Joe Morgan's aide. He instructed him to sit down and continue to apply direct pressure to his shoulder until the paramedics arrived and would take over. The officer assessed that the scene was emergent, but was confused by the very calm, quiet two people in the room who appeared to have this incident strangely under control. Except for the fact that there was a man who was bleeding from a bullet hole punctured in his arm. "What happened here?" The officer already was looking for a statement. Carrie suddenly felt shaky. The gun she had fired was now on the counter that separated her from Joe Morgan and the officer. The officer eyed the gun. He gloved his hands and confiscated it for evidence.

"She had a concealed carry," Joe Morgan began, and Carrie thought, *here we go. I'm going to be locked up for his attempted murder.* "We were talking about safety and what she was doing to protect herself. She showed me the weapon she kept under the counter. Neither one of us knew that it was loaded, and she accidently fired it." Carrie couldn't believe what he was saying. *That was his statement? There would be no charges brought against her? No jail time?*

"Is that true, ma'am?" the officer directed his question at Carrie, as she made a sudden attempt to make up her mind whether or not to go along with his story. If she did not, she would be handcuffed, and arrested, and locked up. Her freedom would be seized. Joe Morgan had threatened her with the fact that he would harm her daughter. No one was going to discover that if Carrie went along with his story. But she really had no other choice. Joe Morgan had her backed into a corner, which apparently was exactly where he wanted her. He was a master manipulator. Any gratitude she may have had toward him for not turning her in was now replaced with fear. The fear of what he wanted from her in return for her freedom. But she took the chance regardless.

Carrie nodded her head, and heard herself say to the officer, "Yes, um, I'm inexperienced. The gun went off unexpectedly." The officer jotted down her statement on a notepad he would use to file this report. With that, the door opened and two paramedics filed in. The focus was on Joe Morgan again. He was hurt. He was bleeding.

Carrie followed behind the ambulance in her SUV. She couldn't just stay at her gallery and resume a work day. She had to know the outcome. Would he need surgery? The officer had stayed behind to sweep the accident scene. Carrie wondered why. If the bullet was still embedded inside of Joe Morgan's shoulder, there was nothing to more to find at that scene other than her gun which she hoped she would never see again. But now, she was in the ER perhaps for the chance to ask Joe Morgan why he lied to the police to protect her.

She watched the ambulance unload the stretcher with him on it. A moment later, Carrie followed them inside of the emergency room. And just as she thought, Tabitha was on duty.

From afar, Carrie saw Tabitha — donned in navy blue scrubs that form fitted her curvy, shapely frame. Within seconds, she made eye contact with the lead paramedic who gave her the rundown of what happened and the status of the patient's vitals. First, she had looked at the shoulder wound. And then Tabitha looked at the face of the patient near her. She instantly stepped back a few steps. She called for another nurse, or someone else on staff with her that could handle this. *Him.*

"I can't," Carrie heard Tabitha say, in no uncertain terms. If she would have finished her statement, Carrie knew Tabitha's reaction would have been along the lines of *I can't help this man because I don't care if he lives or dies.* Well, Carrie cared, because despite however she was provoked, it was her fault that Joe Morgan was currently bleeding to death. Or, he would come close to that, if he didn't seek treatment. Carrie pushed past the paramedic standing closest to Tabitha.

"Carrie? What are you doing here?" The surprise and confusion of this day already had Tabitha's head spinning. Carrie looked down at Joe Morgan on the gurney. Thick gauze covering his shoulder was completely saturated with blood. He had an IV drip going. And she saw a smirk on his face. *Bastard.*

"Long story," Carrie tried to keep her voice down. They were in the ER, and there was a patient that needed Tabitha's attention. There wasn't much time to swap words. Their faces were so close together right now that Carrie could smell the mint gum Tabitha was chewing. And if she wasn't actually chewing it, Carrie knew that it was stored in the pit of one of her gums way in the back of her mouth where she had a wisdom tooth surgically cut out in college. There really wasn't anything they did not know about each other. The same with Beth. "Just help him!" Carrie told her, somewhat frantically. Tabitha frowned. And the lead paramedic lost patience with her and said something in reference to it being *her job to act now!* "I shot him," Carrie said through clenched teeth. Tabitha sprung into action, but not before she told Carrie *not to go anywhere!* What she left unsaid was she wanted an explanation. She needed to know what in the hell happened.

Joe Morgan had a flesh wound. Tabitha was the one who informed him of that while she instructed another nurse to stitch him up. She was done touching him. A prompt x-ray had shown there was no bullet embedded anywhere in the shoulder, tissue, muscle, or bone. The pain and the bleeding were coming from superficial tissue, and after being sewn back together, Joe Morgan would be released. Tabitha had ignored him when he said, twice, to ask her girlfriend how that happened to him. How he ended up with a bullet wound in his arm.

Tabitha was in a rush to get out of that room. She also had a job to do. As she documented the incident on the laptop and what had been done to treat the patient, she prepared his discharge papers. All the while, she and Joe Morgan were left alone.

Her back was to him and her fingers were hurriedly punching the keys. "Aren't you the least bit curious how Mother Teresa ended up shooting me?" He made reference to Carrie as a saint. Ironically, they all did. Most times she was comparable to a do-gooder, but not this time. People obviously could be misread. Tabitha was still dumbfounded.

"I have a job to do," she responded without turning around, but dammit she wanted to know.

"A job that you hesitated to perform until your girlfriend told you to save me." Joe Morgan was entirely too involved in their lives. And that only seemed to be getting worse. Tabitha was terrified of the thought that Carrie could be criminally charged with some type of attempted murder, while Joe Morgan was the one who was evil and immoral. "I appreciate what you did for me today."

"A flesh wound is hardly life-threatening. Sign here," Tabitha shoved a clipboard at him. He took the pen lying on top, and scribbled his signature where he was told.

"When someone puts a bullet in you, it's life threatening. I, however, protected her when the police came and started asking questions." Tabitha stared at him, waiting to hear more, even though he was not the person she wanted to tell her this story. "I'm not pressing charges. It was a case of an inexperienced gun owner not knowing that her weapon was loaded. An accidental fire, as they call it."

Tabitha felt herself breathe a sigh of relief. She was certain that was a lie, or a cover up. She still didn't know what really happened to provoke Carrie to open fire on him, but right here and now she had another question for him.

"After Beth…you were gone from our lives," she boldly stated, "and then you just started showing up here and there. First, you targeted Rory, then myself, and now Carrie?" Tabitha grabbed the clipboard from his lap and the pen fell, and bounced on the floor. She left it untouched. "I want to know what you are after, and why you won't just leave us the hell alone."

"These pain meds are making me really groggy, doc." Joe Morgan purposely closed his eyes.

"I'm a nurse, not a doctor," Tabitha barked at him, and he opened his eyes.

"Either way you're sexy as hell in those scrubs. You're husband is a loser. If you were mine, I'd stop at nothing to protect you from harm." This implication didn't scare Tabitha half as much as it repulsed her.

"From the looks of who came rushing into the ER on a gurney today, I'd say the score is zero on your end. So, you tell me, Morgan, who's the loser?"

Joe Morgan chuckled at her before he shut his eyes for real. The medication had truly kicked in this time. Then Tabitha finally walked out of that room. Still, with no answers.

Chapter Twenty-two

Tabitha was relieved to see the waiting room was vacant, as she hoped for a few minutes alone with Carrie. Carrie stood up as soon as she saw her coming. She reached for Tabitha and openly cried in her arms. Tabitha got close to her ear and whispered. "Tell me what happened to make you shoot him." For the moment, they sat down together. As long as the waiting room stayed empty, they could talk right there.

"I was a shaky mess this morning after I met with my lawyer," Carrie wiped her tears with her fingers. "I'm going ahead with the divorce," Tabitha squeezed her knee as they sat close. That was good news. Tabitha wanted Carrie to grow a backbone, and sustain one with Dom. He no longer deserved her. "I opened the gallery afterward and Joe Morgan came in. I don't know what he even wanted. He was just being his inflammatory self. He brought up Beth. He told me about the last time he saw her." Carrie was trembling, and she began to cry again. Tabitha's impatience for answers grew. "He was the one who put the idea into her head about stabbing herself. He pretty much told her to do it. He said he had done everything to try to break her from him, everything but put a knife in her heart." Those words and that truth sickened Carrie beyond belief.

"That son of a bitch…" Tabitha spoke under her breath. "So that's why you shot him? I mean, I get your anger and how you wanted to avenge Beth's death, but you could have killed him and gone to jail for the rest of your life! Who wins then?"

Carrie shook her head. "No. That's not why. I mean, it really hurt me to know that, but what prompted me to grab for my gun behind the counter was the way he spoke of Jess. He knew too much about my daughter — where she goes to school, her feisty persona, and how she was Beth's godchild. He asked me if the thought of him befriending my daughter rattled me. And he said if not, it should. Tab, I couldn't handle it. If he ever hurt her…" Carrie broke down again.

"So you shot him. Of course you shot him. He's dangerous, and he has this way of making us feel like we have no control over what he's threatening to do. Believe me, Rory gets that just as much as you do." Tabitha completely understood, too, and she was trying to be supportive of the fact that Carrie made a stupid, reckless mistake. It was inconceivable the kind of mind games this man played with people.

"As out of control as picking up that gun was, it gave me an overwhelming sense of power. It happened so fast, but I felt like I was defending Beth, who was never strong enough to shake that bastard. I also was standing on my own two feet for the first time in I don't know how long. Dom's threats and the way he too wants to control me for my decision to end our marriage also was front and center on my mind. I'm tired of being bullied. But most of all, I wanted to keep Jess safe. He started to walk away, he implied that he would find her. I couldn't let that happen."

"Jesus, Carrie. You could have just called the police! You shot him. You shot a man. But not just any man. Joe Morgan!" Tabitha attempted to take in a deep breath. "He told me that he's not pressing charges. Did he really fabricate a story to the police, making it sound like an accident on your part?"

"He did, and apparently the police bought it." Carrie felt convinced of that anyway.

"But this isn't over," Tabitha spoke in no uncertain terms.

And Carrie agreed. "He wants something in return, for sure. I am so afraid of what that might be. It's like I owe him now."

"Let's be realistic," Tabitha spoke, finally feeling as if she had some clarity about all of this. It hadn't hit her before now.

"He doesn't want Rory to deal for him, he doesn't want me, or you, or your child. Those are all ploys for him, or maybe purposeful distractions for us. Joe Morgan goes big or he goes home. And there's only one thing that's big. It could explain why he's let several months go by since Beth died. She would have just turned forty, remember?"

Carrie sat up straighter on her chair and the two of them turned inward toward each other until their knees touched. "Do you think she told him?"

"I think we know that Beth became someone else entirely when she was with him. She lost all perspective. Obviously, at the end, she lost her mind over him. It's very possible that she told him in an effort to hold onto him, to prolong keeping him in her life," Tabitha had drawn a conclusion that had not thought of before. And it made sense.

"But it didn't work," Carrie stated, feeling confused. "Right? I mean, if she confided in him, he still pushed her away countless times, and then he implied for her in the most cruel, hurtful terms, to end her life. Do you really think he knew what she was worth?"

Tabitha pondered for a moment. "That's just it. Beth wasn't worth three and a half million dollars. That trust wasn't entitled to her until she turned forty years old."

That was the way her grandmother had arranged it. But in the event of Beth's untimely death, her grandmother's fortune could be in limbo if she had not allocated an alternate plan, or beneficiary. Beth had no living will intact when she took her own life at thirty-nine years old. That was the extent of what Tabitha and Carrie knew about her fortune. And because she had no family left, Carrie and Tabitha had sorted through her apartment and divvied up the memories. So many of her sentimental material things, they kept between the two of them. Other miscellaneous things, they had donated to charity. Also donated was the money Beth had in one bank account. Tabitha and Carrie had agreed to contribute the fifteen grand of Beth's money to dementia research, given that was how Beth had lost her grandmother five years prior. The two of them had been close, but Tabitha and Carrie never liked the way Beth's grandmother pushed her to find a man and start a family. Even as far back as when they were in college together. But, that was the one stipulation of the trust fund. Beth would see no amount of money from the trust fund until five years after the date she was married, and she was required to have at least one child by then. If she had remained unmarried and motherless, the terms of the trust stated that Beth would not receive the three and half million dollars until she reached the age of forty. Beth once halfheartedly joked with both Tabitha and Carrie about how her grandmother must have considered a woman, by forty, who was single and unattached, to be an old maid. Beth never cared at all about the money, but Tabitha and Carrie were suddenly concerned that Joe Morgan did.

There were unanswered questions. Beth's would-be fortieth birthday had come and gone. Tabitha and Carrie had not inquired about the trust, because neither one of them cared about the millions of dollars that Beth rarely spoke of and appeared to not have given a second thought. Her years spent searching for a husband and yearning for children were genuine, and not at all about greed. If it had been, they knew

Beth would have stayed in her unhappy first marriage right out of college. The two of them didn't want the money that was once in Beth's name. They missed her dearly, and only wanted to preserve her memory, and their wonderful times with her. Not her questionable fortune.

"I just have one serious worry right now," Tabitha spoke to Carrie. "What if there was some sort of change in that trust? What if, in case of death, Beth had arranged for that money to go to Joe Morgan? What if he has been sniffing around us for information? Maybe he thinks we have her money? Maybe he thinks he can force us to lead him to his money…if Beth promised it to him."

"Tab, what if his motive to push her to suicide wasn't just about getting her out of his life—"

"Exactly what I'm thinking, too. Because he wanted her money all to himself!" Together they came to a conclusion that sickened them. Beth's life mattered. So much had changed in how they grieved now. This wasn't about accepting that Beth had taken her life because she had gotten caught up in a man who didn't want her. This, indirectly, was about murder. And how Joe Morgan would stop at nothing to get what he wanted.

Chapter Twenty-three

Carrie didn't know where to start when Dom came home in time for dinner. She had to tell him about the shooting — and the fact that she filed for divorce from him that morning. She sent the girls to the movies again, having prearranged their plans and their ride. Jess called her out on trying to get rid of them, and Carrie refrained from scolding her. She merely agreed, and told her that sometimes parents need some time alone to discuss important things. Sheridan was worried about her mother. To her, there seemed to be more going on than Carrie was willing to tell them. And she was absolutely right.

"I didn't cook," was the first thing she told him when he walked into the kitchen. *Why had she felt like she still needed to take care of him?* "The girls split a frozen pizza and left for the movies — because we need to talk." Dom never responded if he wanted to eat. He only slipped off his suit jacket and hung it over the back of one of the kitchen chairs before he sat down on it. Carrie was already seated directly in front of him. "I'm not sure where to start," she began. She still felt shaky from all that had happened in one day.

"You can start by telling me that deciding to file for divorce is not what you really want," Dom told her. He knew. Carrie wasn't sure how he found out, but it saddened her already that he had not heard it directly from her.

"I can't stay married to you, not after what you've done." Plain and simple. There was no going back. No saving or resurrecting their love — and trust.

"I want this to be as amicable as possible, for our sake and especially for the girls." Carrie held her breath. She wished with all of her heart that Dom would give up his ridiculous quest to take everything from her. She believed her attorney and now had great hope that Dom could not overrule her. She was owed half of everything, and at least joint custody. More, if she chose to fight dirty.

"Of course you do. I'm sure you hired a lawyer that promised you the moon and stars when it comes to all I'm worth. You're going to be in for a rude awakening though, honey. I can hire the shadiest team of attorneys to win this settlement. You're going to be left with nothing. The girls not only will stay in this house with me, but they want to. You would think that fact alone would make you change your mind. But, since it hasn't, it makes me wonder if I've misread you as a mother."

"Fuck you!" Carrie spat at him in anger.

"Someone has been spending too much time with her foul-mouthed friend. Her manners are rubbing off on you." Dom insulted Tabitha.

"Why are you doing this?" Carrie asked him.

"I want you to see that we don't have to lose our marriage. I made a mistake. I regret what I did more than you will ever know. I know you find this difficult to understand because you've never done a damn thing wrong in your entire life. You're good and honest and so pure. But, sometimes, most of us are tempted to veer off track and do something wild — or wrong."

"Stop making me out to be some sort of saint. I know what it's like to choose tempting, and I especially understand the repercussions of doing something out of control." The raw image from just several hours ago flashed into her mind. She fired a gun at Joe Morgan. "I have to tell you something, Dom." He immediately wondered if his wife had an affair. It would pain him to know that, but if she had, it would oddly make their marriage easier to mend. They would both have something to forgive and forget. "Joe Morgan showed up at the gallery today." Dom frowned. "He's a dangerous man. He made some serious threats."

"Toward you? Did he hurt you?" Dom demanded answers. The thought of her scared or hurt at the hands of that man appeared to affect him.

"No. But he repeatedly mentioned Jess. He brought up things he knew about her, including that she attends Hays Middle School. He told me he was going after her."

"You called the police, right!" Dom was in an instant state of panic.

"The police were called, yes," she answered, "after I shot him."

"You did what!" Dom was aware she owned a gun that she strictly kept stored at the gallery. "With your handgun?" Carrie nodded. "Holy Christ! What happened? Is he dead?" If that was a fact, Dom wondered why his wife wasn't behind bars, preparing to plead self defense or anything else to regain her freedom.

"He only has a flesh wound to his shoulder," Carrie stated. "He was treated and released from the emergency room."

"And how is it that you are here? Did you call someone else for bail money? Jesus, Carrie. You should have reached out to me. I am still your husband."

"Joe Morgan didn't press charges. In fact, he told the police that it was an accidental shooting. He made up a story about me being inexperienced with my own weapon, and that I didn't realize the gun was loaded."

"Why did he do that? What does he want in return?" Dom still looked startled.

"I have no idea." That was only partly true. But Carrie had promised Tabitha that she wouldn't speak of the trust in Beth's name. Not until they enlisted Rory's help to find out if the trust still existed and if any changes had been made to it.

"I want the girls home tonight!" he panicked. "And I want to protect you, too."

"We will be at the movies when it's over tonight to pick them up. And when we get home, we will tell the girls that Joe Morgan could be a danger to all of us. They don't have to know exactly what happened, and we will not put any fear into Jess in particular. She and Sheridan both do need to be aware of how important it is for them to keep their eyes open to their surroundings." Dom seemed at ease with Carrie's suggestion. He also liked that she hadn't objected to him wanting to protect her. As a husband would. And he hoped to use it to his advantage.

Rory did his research after Tabitha called him from the hospital to share the latest Joe Morgan saga. At first, he thought he heard her wrong. *Carrie shot the man? Carrie Tyler?* But he certainly understood that when it came to push and shove at the hands of Joe Morgan, he never left anyone still standing. Even though Carrie managed to shoot him, he manipulated the outcome for her to be indebted to him. The man was a monster.

Tabitha sat down at the kitchen island. She was drinking a glass of wine before their dinner that Rory already had baking in the oven. Her alcohol intake had not changed since he expressed his disapproval of her habit weeks ago. What had changed was Rory stopped verbalizing about it.

He told her that he made a few phone calls and quickly discovered it can be beyond difficult to find out if a trust existed. One of the advantages of creating a trust was that it's private — it does not actually have to be recorded or published. He was told the best way to find a trust was to ask the person who created it, or the person who managed it. Rory struck out on both accounts. Beth's grandmother was deceased. And whoever managed the trust for her could have been anyone. Possibly anyone in Hays, though, which narrowed his search down to somewhat impossible instead of utterly impossible. He learned that living trusts do not have to be made public record because they do not go through probate. This entire search was out of Rory's hands because both the beneficiary and the settlor of the trust had died. Because the trust was monetary only, and had not been in the form of real estate or any traceable materialistic items, it apparently was not recorded.

"So that's it?" Tabitha concluded from Rory's findings. "There's no way for us to find Beth's trust, which also means there's no way for us to stop Joe Morgan from getting his hands on that money — if his name was added in some way before Beth died."

"I doubt that his name was anywhere on it," Rory spoke in no uncertain terms. "I think it's likely that he knows about the millions of dollars that Beth was supposed to inherit. Did you ever think that maybe Beth added, in the precautionary event of her death, that she wanted both you and Carrie to be the beneficiaries since she had no family left? And maybe Joe Morgan was aware of that."

"Which could also explain why he's not leaving me or Carrie alone, and why he's targeting our family members," Tabitha concluded. "So what do we do? Confront him?"

"Absolutely not, because we may be way off." Rory didn't want Joe Morgan anywhere near his wife, or his family. Carrie and her children included.

"Right, the last thing we want to do is give him more leverage."

Rory shook his head in agreement. And while he wished no ill will on Carrie, he thought about how their lives would have instantly changed for the better if she'd had a sweeter aim.

Chapter Twenty-four

"You do know who that sweetheart is, don't you?" The bartender at Gutch's asked Joe Morgan once Beth stepped away to use the restroom. It was the night they met at the bar and shared the pizza that was supposed to be for Beth's take-out, but she had spontaneously offered to dine with him, with the hope that they could get to know each other.

"Beth Louden, a social worker downtown Hays. A woman looking to settle down, that part is obvious," Joe Morgan recited what he knew, and sipped the last of the beer in his glass before he pushed it away on the bar top.

"Her grandmother and my Nana were tight. I remember Beth, living with her grandmother. She's older than me. She was smokin' hot in short shorts when I was nine and she was probably nineteen."

"She doesn't remember you?" Joe Morgan asked the bartender.

"I guess I have too much facial hair now," he joked, and they chuckled. "Everyone knows that Beth's grandmother was the original curator of the Hays Arts Council. It's what she was about. Through the years, when the program would lose state funds, she would keep it going from her own pocket. Anyway, the woman was like an heir or something and had tucked a few million in a trust for her only granddaughter. But the strange catch was she had to be married for five years and have given birth to at least one baby in order to cash in the money. Beth is neither. But that marriage and baby deal expires when she's forty and then the trust is hers. I once asked what would happen to the money if Beth didn't make it to forty, you know, sadly people die young, as her parents did. Nana didn't have any particular answer, other than Beth probably was given the right to have someone closest to her listed as a secondary beneficiary." The bartender stopped talking and turned to refill the empty beer glass for him. He spotted Beth on her way back from the powder room.

She sat back down on the bar stool right next to him. He seized her up. He wasn't the marrying kind. But Joe Morgan was a man who always liked to have a plan, as he now had for Beth Louden, the heiress.

Beth tried entirely too hard for months on end to get him to commit. And he would waver back and forth between being interested in her, and not. He was cautious to keep his *side business* from her. The number of times she had seen him with a Yeti were lost to him, but she had never caught on that he was selling opioid to every druggie in Hays. And still, he was greedy for more money. Beth's inheritance was never brought up. She hadn't told him, and then six months into their relationship — Joe Morgan asked.

They were lying naked in his bed. The sex was explosive between them, and always seemed to draw him back to her one more time. She was talking to him, she was always speaking of or analyzing something. It drove him batshit crazy, but he had learned how to pretend to listen. She brought up when she was a little girl and having been raised by her grandmother. And suddenly Joe Morgan was actually listening.

"You know, babe…" he pinched the nipple of one of her full, bare breasts. "Hays has over twenty-thousand people but somehow everyone still knows each other, and their business." He could see in her eyes how much she loved it when he talked to her, when he didn't just nod along to appease her when she was looking for meaningful conversation with him. "I mentioned to a buddy of mine that we're seeing each other." Beth smiled, and touched the scruff on his face. He brought her fingers to his lips and softly kissed them. He could see how those moments of affection exemplified how taken she was with him. The times that he pretended to be genuine, and love her.

"You told a friend that I'm yours?" The flattery radiated off of her face.

"Absolutely, I did. And as I said, people know people here. He said he remembered you, apparently you were nineteen and he was somewhat younger but he can recall your sexy long legs in short shorts." Beth threw her head back and laughed. "His granny apparently was chummy with yours."

"Really? What's her name?"

"No idea, she's long passed away," he covered with a lie for his story. "So is it true that you have a trust in waiting, worth quite a chunk of change?"

Beth looked him straight in the eyes. "Yes." She didn't freely share that fact with just anyone. Being a social worker was not a profession she had chosen for fortune, or glory. She saw it as being rich with meaning. A place where she would have the power to make a difference. She was drawn to fighting for the well-being of others. She didn't need money to be happy. And a part of her wondered what would happen once she turned forty years old and suddenly had a hefty bank account. She would certainly consider charities that needed the money more than she did. And when she mentioned that concept to Joe Morgan, he all but rolled his eyes.

"You never talk about your extended family," he began, and he thought of two of her closest friends who annoyed him beyond tolerance. "You probably have some pissed off first or second cousins who expected to be named in that trust..."

Beth shook her head. Her long dark hair fell over one shoulder and partially covered her naked chest. Her skin was porcelain. Her eyes were crystal blue. She was a beauty. And one day she would be an incredibly rich beauty. "Just me. My grandmother and I are all each other had for most of my life. Until I met my girlfriends in college. Tabitha and Carrie are my sisters by heart." Joe Morgan had his answer. Those two bitches were named as next in line beneficiaries — if something were to unfortunately happen to Beth.

"Well I'm glad you found them," he offered, but didn't mean those words in the least.

"Me too," she smiled.

"You're a rare gem, Elizabeth," he complimented her as the tightness grew between his legs again. "I'm not going to lie, money turns me on." She giggled at his size beneath the sheets. "But, a woman who cares about everything and everyone above it, draws me in more." He kissed her full on the mouth. She was touched by his words. For him to understand that about her, meant the world to her. She responded to his passionate kiss. "Maybe one day I'll mean enough to you to be listed as a beneficiary..." he spoke in nearly a whisper as he pressed his body closer to hers. She thought about what he said as he began to make love to her again. He was over top of her, and she spoke as she ran her fingers through his dark hair. "That won't be necessary, because by then you'll be my husband and we'll share everything." He concealed how he cringed at her implication. And he caught her by surprise when he unexpectedly entered her and began to rock over her body.

Joe Morgan still had time to change her mind, as he knew Beth was only thirty-eight years old.

Chapter Twenty-five

"Tell them no." Tabitha was adamant. There was no possible way that Rory Chance had it in him to pull off going undercover for the Hays Police Department. They were impatient to catch Joe Morgan and bring down his apparent city-wide drug ring, and the detectives on the case had sought Rory's help. He was going to appear desperate for work, and Joe Morgan was supposed to buy into that.

"I can't tell them no. I am shocked that you would even ask me to, considering how much you loathe the man for everything that he's done." And for who he had taken away from her.

"He's too smart. He'll be onto you and you're going to get yourself killed!" Tabitha had just gotten home from work. She stood in the kitchen, still wearing her navy blue scrubs. She wanted a drink and instantly moved to the refrigerator in search of a bottle of wine."

"Yeah, great, just great, drinking will help!" Rory threw up his hands and rolled his eyes. There was no sign that dinner was cooked. Rory had spent the last hour on the phone with one of the detectives from the Hays PD.

Damn right, Tabitha thought, as she poured herself a full glass of white wine. She took a drink before she spoke to him again. "I don't like this, Rory." She didn't know what else to say. She could have cried as she imagined it all going down wrong. Police back-up or not, Rory would be putting himself smack in the middle of serious danger with thugs who didn't care who lived or died.

"Where's my adventurous, risk-taker wife?" Rory asked her, as he smiled at her. She had always been the one to dive in the deep water. To hell with feet first in the shallow end. When Rory gave her his name on the day they married, he told her he believed it was fittingly perfect for her. *Tabitha Chance.* "You've never passed on taking a chance — uncertain or definite. You've always just done it, or seized it."

"I've never had so much at stake before," she told him. "You're my husband, the father of my boys. We are a family. Party of four. If you don't know how much we need you, then you're a dumbass."

Rory chuckled. "I've been called worse." And Tabitha attempted to smile.

"I recall you, not so long ago, being scared out of your mind when Joe Morgan had you trapped, forced into doing something illegal and downright frightening. Even after we went to the police, you still wanted to back out of pretending to be a part of that network of criminals. What gives? What's any different this time?"

"Our lives are in limbo as long as he's free. His reminder — or no, his warning, to you in the parking lot to be ready, he's coming for you — is enough to make me lose my mind. What happens the next time you and Carrie plan a girls night and stay out until the wee hours of the morning? Or what if you're alone at the gym? He's going to show up somewhere and I don't want to know what that feels like when you don't come home."

"Exactly," Tabitha spoke quietly. "To reiterate your words, I don't want to know what it feels like when *you* don't come home."

Rory took her in his arms and held her close. He tightened his arms around her. He wanted to tell her that everything was going to be okay. But he didn't.

Carrie was in her bedroom getting ready. She wasn't slipping into her usual casual clothes to throw a paint apron overtop later. She had chosen a pair of semi-fitted black dress pants with a high low pale pink sweater. She was slipping into a pair of black wedges in her enormous walk-in closet when Dom came in there and stood next to her. He was already dressed for work, and Carrie had actually thought he left the house, or was downstairs making coffee to-go.

"You look nice," he told her, but it didn't feel like a compliment. Those days were long gone between them. It just appeared as if he noticed she was dressed up, or different. "Not going painting today?" *Going painting.* It sounded demeaning, as if she was a child taking part in playtime. Maybe her husband had always made her feel that way. She wasn't certain, nor did she even care anymore.

"No, I have a meeting this morning," Carrie responded, but refrained to mention that it was with her divorce attorney.

"I've heard good things about Kristie Weh. She's a fierce act in the courtroom. She's pro-women. But this is one case where she will have to succumb to loss from a man."

"You're not acting much like a man these days," Carrie replied, and the moment she said it, she felt regretful. But she was still so very hurt and angry.

"That's low, Carrie. I told you, it's over."

"Even if it is over and done, you can't change the fact that you did it. You broke us. I'm not going to pick up those pieces. I'm walking away with my dignity and my pride."

"All alone?" he asked her, "because that's what you'll be. My team of lawyers already have a case built. They'll start with the time you forgot to pick up the girls at school, and continue with all the nights you spent in your studio while you're eleven-year-old little girls were home alone." That was inaccurate and unfair. There were many evenings she had dropped off the girls for volleyball practice and saw to it that they had a ride home, if she wasn't going to be there to pick them up herself. But most times she was their chauffer. If the girls were ever home alone for any amount of time, it was because Dom was expected to be there but never seemed to make it home from work at a decent hour. Dom was painting his own picture. An image that depicted his wife as an unfit, uncaring mother.

Carrie shook her head at him, in disgust. "That's your dirty plan, huh?" She all but laughed at him. "Funny how you are so confident that I am going to be portrayed as all bad, when you are the one who did something pretty awful to your wife, and your family. Your girls will find out someday, someday when they are women and able to understand that life's choices do make or break us."

"You're too good, Carrie. People like you get walked all over. I want to instill in our girls to stand up for themselves." Again, he was demeaning her.

"Are you pushing me to ruin you? Your reputation? Your daddy-of-the-year status?"

Dom chuckled, obviously mocking her. He was not the man she fell in love with, and shared so many years with. At this point in their unraveling marriage, she was not even sure she loved him at all anymore. Carrie did realize that he was acting out of fear. But hurting her was only pushing her further away from him. He was right. She would never stoop so low as to ruin his image in their children's eyes. But she would save herself from losing. She may have been the good girl most of her life. But she wasn't a fool.

She pushed past him inside of their walk-in closet that had his and her things stored on separate sides. It was strange how standing in that closet, so divided with his clothing and shoes versus everything of hers, mirrored how separated and on opposite sides the two of them now were.

"Where are you going?" Dom's voice sounded panicked, as if he feared she was about to storm into their daughter's rooms and blurt out the truth about their father to them.

Carrie retrieved her cell phone from the nightstand near her side of the bed. She had not slept in their bed with him, or there at all, since the night she discovered him *and his secret* in his office. She turned around to look directly at him. "The night that I made my way up to the fifth floor of your office building, I saw Steve Radloff. You know, at all the Christmas parties and functions that you dragged me to through the years, I used to chat it up with Steve. He's a nice guy." Carrie watched Dom roll his eyes. He never did like that certain co-worker of his. They challenged each other too much, Carrie thought, and had always tried to outdo the other. "I think Steve crushes on me. He sent me a text last week…"

"Are you contemplating sleeping with Steve? Is this your payback, Carrie?"

"Oh no. I'm not interested in sleeping with anyone. I just wanted to share with you that I know Steve works late, just like you." Carrie turned her phone around so he could see one of the seven photos that she had stored on her cell-phone and backed up on disk. "It's over? That's what you said. It seems that Steve overheard your plan to divorce me and leave me with absolutely nothing. He felt sorry for me. Or maybe, he wanted to one up you in a really big way. From the angle of the photos I received, it looks like Steve was standing on the other side of that cracked office door just like I was when my knees shook and my heart shattered."

Dom started to pace in front of her. "You are not going to use those against me in court." He referred to the indecent photos of himself with Rob.

"You lied to me, and you continue to lie to me," she told him. "This fling, or this new direction that you obviously want to take your private life in, is a high for you. I know how you get when you are obsessed with something. You cannot very easily back away, or cut your ties. I've seen you be that way year after year in your career, and with your family. I am standing here as your wife. You don't want me anymore, but you can't seem to let go of what we had. You think you can still control me. You think I'm still yours." Carrie paused. She watched him, and his silence told her that he was finally listening. "I'm going to give you the chance to drop your team of lawyers, to stop your false accusations of me. And if you don't, I will fight you with the truth. These photos will go public, your reputation will be tarnished, and your girls will eventually find out — but I promise you it will not be from me."

"What do you want?" he asked her, and his face was one of a man she no longer recognized. He looked defeated. And that was not Dominic Tyler.

"Shared custody of our girls." Her answer should not have amazed him. She was a woman of character. A woman that he had been lucky to have by his side. Her words next, however, did take him by surprise. "We will sell the house, and we will divvy up everything in it. This house will be left behind as a memory for our family of four. No one lives here alone with our girls. Not you, and not me. Separately, we will give them new lives, new memories, in two different homes.

Dom relented. He backed down. He agreed. "I had you wrong. All wrong," he spoke with a shaky voice, and his face was flushed. She could see the beads of perspiration on top of his nose. "You're savvy. You know how to hold your own and get what you want."

"Dom," she spoke his name with slight endearment again. "I had what I wanted. You and our girls. And now, I just want them, and the chance to make a new life."

He nodded. He agreed. He relented. And after fifteen years, that was the end of Mr. and Mrs. Tyler and their family of four.

Chapter Twenty-six

Rory met with the detectives of the Hays PD before he was guided, step by step, how to approach Joe Morgan. A few back and forth texts between Rory and Joe Morgan were monitored, and the police believed they had him right where they wanted him. Tabitha was the only one who wasn't convinced. She believed that it was too soon to act, and she was unconvinced they could ever deceive a man like Joe Morgan.

Rory: I know you threatened my wife in the parking lot that night.

Joe Morgan: It wasn't a threat. It was a friendly reminder. If you had done what you were paid well to do, you wouldn't be panicking like a scared little boy right now.

Rory: Leave my wife alone!

Joe Morgan: You're going to have to do more than hide behind your phone.

Rory was instructed by the police not to reply, only to wait to see if he had more to add, or offer.

Joe Morgan: Find a job yet?

Rory: No.

Joe Morgan: I never give a nark a second chance, but you've got one if you're man enough.

Rory: I don't want to do your dirty work. I want you to leave my wife alone.

Joe Morgan: You can't have both.

Rory: I want your word that you will drop your threat.

Joe Morgan: You first. Prove yourself. The upfront pay is 2 grand again. The Yeti will be in the back lot of Donnewald, behind the building, at the loading dock at midnight.

Rory: I never said yes to this.

Joe Morgan: Then I'll take your sanity before I take your wife.

Rory was again instructed not to respond, to say nothing more to Joe Morgan. He would just drive up to the loading dock at midnight and expect to be given further instructions from there. The police believed another insulated cup would lead them one person closer to Joe Morgan. Rory was on board. It was as if he had a purpose again, outside of being there for his family, day in and day out. Tabitha could see the fire in his eyes. He didn't appear the least bit afraid, as he had the last time the police and he worked to bring down the drug traffickers. And that unnerved her.

"This time you're staying put," Rory reminded her, as the clocked showed half past eleven. She watched him put her car keys in the front pocket of his denim to ensure she could not leave. "Please just stay safe."

"And what about you? You're not safe. You're walking into something so explosive and the fact that you can't see that pisses me off so bad!"

Rory smiled at her. She was explosive. His firecracker. And God he loved her. "I see it, but I also see this as if something goes wrong, the police are there. The last time I was so freaked out, and it all played out smoothly. I really don't have to do much. Just drive up. Find the Yeti, and text Morgan for the delivery destination. I doubt he will be anywhere in plain sight. He's not stupid."

"So beforehand the police will catch him, or someone else, on camera, placing that Yeti near the loading dock?"

"That might have already happened. I don't know, I have not heard," Rory told her. It all seemed poorly planned to her. Joe Morgan had supposedly gotten away with dealing drugs for years. He could, and he would, outsmart everyone again.

Tabitha watched him grab for his cell phone and his own set of truck keys off the island's countertop. "I will call you as soon as it's over and I'm headed back home."

"Hurry, okay? Be safe, you hear me?" Her eyes clouded with tears. When she wanted to be strong it sometimes backfired.

Rory took her into his arms and pulled her close. "I will, I promise." He kissed her on the forehead, nose, and lips. And then he walked out the door. Tabitha wanted to call out to him one more time. To have him turn around and look at her. Pull her close again. But she wouldn't go there in her mind. This was not going to be the last time.

Rory's truck engine had not even turned over in the garage yet, when Tabitha was on her phone. She sent one text message. *"Pick me up."* And Carrie replied she was on her way.

From the passenger seat of Carrie's full-size SUV, Tabitha rooted through her handbag in search of a flask. And she found it.

"What are you doing? Are you seriously drinking wine in my vehicle?" Carrie looked to the side and spoke to Tabitha without keeping her eyes on the dark road in front of her.

"No, it's vodka. I'm sorry, honey. I need something to take the edge off."

"Yeah, I do too, but I'm driving. Tab, I want this to be over with him just as much as you do. Remember he threatened my girl, and I lost it!"

Tabitha nodded her head mid swallow. Straight vodka had momentarily left a burning sensation on her tongue and down her throat. "He needs to be out of our lives, but I'm so afraid that Rory isn't as safe as he thinks he is tonight."

"And just how are we going to stay out of sight so we don't hinder the set-up?" Carrie asked. She was ready and willing to help Tabitha. That would never change in their lives together. She just hoped she had plan. And knowing Tabitha, she always did.

As he was told, Rory prepared to text Joe Morgan as soon as his truck rolled on the grounds of Donnewald Distributing. But before he could send that text, he received one.

Good decision. Drive around back. Park close to the dock. Leave your truck running, headlights on. The Yeti is on the deck's south side, underneath the second step. Your wadded payment is taped to it. Get it, get back into your truck. Wait for headlights. The buyer will park nose to nose with your truck. Get out, meet him halfway to exchange the Yeti for the payment, in sync. These guys are pros. Be ready and be confident. Don't screw this up.

The text was long, and Rory drove across the graveled lot as he read it word for word. The pick-up and delivery were happening at the same spot. He was frazzled and nervous now. The deal was about to get real. He had only hoped his agreement with the police would remain intact. If anything were to happen to him, Tabitha would need protection from that maniac. Rory forwarded the message to the detective in charge of this plan tonight. Instantly, a reply came through, and it was confirmed that the police were already on the grounds.

Rory took a deep breath and repeatedly reassured himself of the fact that trained officers were there, staked out, in the distance. They were wearing night vision goggles and armed with sniper rifles.

He made it to the step on the loading dock, and with the flashlight on his cell phone, he retrieved the Yeti from hole in the ground that held it upright. He tore off the wad of taped cash and pocketed it. The insulated cup didn't feel nearly as weighted as the last one he held. In fact, it felt as if it was liquid. Rory had no idea if opioid even existed in liquid form. He didn't care to know either. This would be his last time doing this, he decided then and there. It was law enforcement's final chance to nail Joe Morgan with his help. If they failed, he would find a way to stop Joe Morgan himself. *Perhaps Carrie had the right idea with putting a bullet in him.*

Rory pounced back onto the seat of his truck and slammed the door closed. His heart was pounding inside of his chest, and he finally was able to take a deep breath. Then the tone of his cell phone startled him.

Carrie parked on the street adjacent to Donnewald, and she and Tabitha had walked the length of the parking lot and around to the side of the building which had the loading dock located behind it. Tabitha had been prepared and driven through there in the daylight that morning, just to be sure of where they would be going in the dark. They walked in silence, with their arms linked. They had agreed to keep their eyes and ears open to keep each other safe. They finally, both breathless, stood and peered from around the side of the building. They could see the headlights of Rory's truck, and the roar of the diesel engine was loud out there in the still night air.

Rory read the text. Another one from Joe Morgan. *Rounding the corner now.*

Sure enough, Rory saw another dark-painted truck, equally as large and loud as his, headed through the back lot. It came to a stop nose to nose with him, just as he was told it would. There was a fair amount of space for them to stand in the beams. Rory reached for the door handle and waited. When he saw the other person's driver's side door open, he too moved to exit.

A figure with a dark hooded sweatshirt walked toward him. Rory was so nervous he could have bent forward and puked on his own shoes. He stood almost toe to toe with a man at least ten years younger than him. No words were spoken. Rory saw the wad of cash in his hand. Rory extended the insulated cup toward the man who only stared back at him. They made the exchange without speaking a word.

Rory turned to leave. The other guy, he assumed, had turned around also. It was strange not to speak, but clearly neither one of them were there to make small talk. Rory had only taken a few steps away when he heard him go down. Nothing could make a man fall flat, face down, that rapidly unless he shot was down. Rory screamed, and a moment later a bullet, coming from the direction of the loading dock steps, hit him square in the chest. His hand met the excruciating, piercing pain that had just ripped through his upper body. He heard screams, which he thought for a moment were Tabitha's. But that couldn't be. He too fell to the gravel. The undercover officers were quick to run to him. The shots ceased after the gunman had taken two men down. Despite the probability of danger, Tabitha took off running to him. She never gave a second thought to being in the line of fire. Carrie had tried to force her back, to hold onto her, to no avail. She gave up fighting her then, and ran after her. It was a risk she too would take. For her best friend. Tabitha had been right. Joe Morgan's only plan tonight was to harm Rory, and anyone else involved.

Out of nowhere, an officer grabbed Tabitha first and then Carrie, and forced them both on the ground in an attempt to protect them if the shooter wasn't done. Lights around the entire back of the building came on, and at least two armed officers chased down the person making a desperate attempt to escape from beneath the steps of the loading dock. *Rory had been that close to the gunman.* Tabitha was only a few feet away from Rory now, as she saw him lay lifeless on his back. She twisted away from the officer to go to him. She heard someone on a two-way radio calling for emergency. *Two men down. Gunshots. Wounded. One in the back, the other in the chest.* She heard another on the scene speaking of how it was *only coffee in place of the drugs. Morgan was nowhere to be found. Someone, presumably the shooter, was being pursued on foot.* She forced herself to block out the voices and the foreign sounds around her. She only cared about him. Saving him. Loving him. Living the rest of her life with him.

"Rory!" she choked out his name in a panic, in an effort to get him to hear her and to open his eyes. She would have given anything, absolutely anything at all, to see that lopsided grin of his right now. The blood on his chest was pooling. She ripped off her sweater to apply pressure to the wound. Left wearing only a camisole on the top half of her body, Tabitha bent over him. Her mind went there quickly. The night she knelt over Beth. The massive amount of blood. The shallow breathing. The god-awful goodbye. *This was going to be different. His life would be spared.* She heard the ambulance sirens in the distance. How many times in a given day, throughout all of those long twelve-hour shifts, had she heard those same sirens. She saved lives every single day. But this man was her life. "Stay with me! You're going to be just fine." *I told you,* she thought, *dammit, you asshole, I warned you!* She recalled the first time she met him. *Rory Chance.* She instantly had wanted to *take a chance* on him. The likelihood of him being the one for her felt strong, and just as intense as the initial spark they shared and sustained between them. Once glance. One touch. And the rest was a part of history in their love story. She could see him rolling up, confident and sexy, straddling his motorcycle, for their first official date. She thought of how that cycle was no longer theirs anymore. *Gone. Never to be seen again. Gone.* Tabitha was losing him. She could feel him slipping away as she fell back onto her bottom and stared blindly as the paramedics pushed their way in and took over. All the while she could feel Carrie's arms wrapped tightly around her, rocking her back and forth. And whispering, *"It's okay. It's okay... it's okay."*

Chapter Twenty-seven

"It's okay." Tabitha turned to Carrie. They stood side-by-side in front of a gravestone marked with such finality. A birthdate. A deathdate. And a name etched in stone. Forever. That marker would weather, but hundreds of years later it would still somehow be legible. Carrie knew how uncomfortable cemeteries made Tabitha. This was actually the first time they had come there together. *Beth Louden.* Subtract the dates separated by a dash and calculate that she had almost lived four decades. "It's okay for us to come here to remember her. We could talk to her. Maybe we should tell her what's been going on, and what we now know for sure."

"I believe she knows," Tabitha spoke for certain. "I'm confident that she somehow saw for herself as justice was finally brought to Joe Morgan." The shooter was captured that night and had shockingly broken down and revealed his boss. He accepted a plea bargain. He made the choice to save his own skin, exactly as Joe Morgan had done countless times. He was Joe Morgan's right-hand man. He knew precisely where to lead the police. He knew all of the covert nooks and crannies, and never-suspected hideways for the opioid. There was enough evidence to bring multiple criminal charges against him, including first degree murder. A life was lost that night. And Joe Morgan would be a very old man when his prison term was up.

A bark from what appeared to be a stray dog alongside of the road near the cemetery caught their attention.

"There's another one for Bethie to save," Carrie noted, and smiled. Tabitha nodded her head in agreement and let out a slight giggle. She had been walking through her own neighborhood just weeks ago when she met up with a woman she recognized as a life-long Hays resident. She crossed paths with her numerous times throughout the years. She also had been in the ER once with her elderly husband. She had to have been every bit of seventy-five years old and still actively out walking her Labrador. That day, she approached Tabitha.

"What your friend did was nothing short of selfless and so wonderful for all of the animals, especially dogs like mine here. I adopted him from the shelter. You know, the nonprofit shelter clear across town?"

Tabitha had heard it was on the verge of closing in recent years, due to insufficient funds, but she hadn't paid much attention to it. *"I'm sorry. You must have me confused with someone else."* Tabitha tried to be polite.

"Oh no. I'm speaking of the social worker, Beth Louden. She wanted to remain anonymous but those at the animal shelter boast her name every chance they get." Tabitha still had not understood. *"She left a trust to the shelter, over three million dollars. They received it just a few weeks ago. Apparently she loved animals that much."*

That she did, Tabitha had thought, as she felt incredible pride fill up her heart. Beth had done the right thing. A good, lasting thing. And now her memory lived on.

"I miss her so much," Tabitha said, looking down at the ground where Beth's body was buried beneath their feet.

Carrie nodded, and fought back the tears. "She's always going to be with us. Feel her? I can."

Tabitha momentarily closed her eyes and smiled. "Yeah, I can, too. But, I hate death. I hate the emptiness and the loss that rips through your body every single day, knowing their presence is no more and their soul has gone on." Carrie wrapped an arm around Tabitha's shoulders and pulled her close.

"It sucks beyond words," Carrie began, "but we still have each other. Beth never would have left if she hadn't been certain of that."

They stood there for awhile longer, sharing silence and swapping loving and encouraging words in a place that felt as sad and as hopeless as you allowed it. When the sun began to set, they hugged near their vehicles before they separately drove away.

As she rolled her car over the curb on her driveway, Tabitha reached to signal her garage door to open. It was a single door to a space wide enough for double cars. The door was halfway up off of the ground when she noticed it. In front of her, in the space ahead of her where she was about to park her car, there was that old Suzuki DR-350 dirt bike. Rory stood beside it, smiling wide, and looking as happy and surprised as she felt. Tabitha hurried to shift her vehicle into park on the driveway and she ran to him and met him in the middle of the garage. "You got it back!" She was careful not to hurt him as she fell into his open embrace. He was still recovering from a bullet to his chest cavity.

"I had to. It's a part of us, and our story."

And their story was far from over.

About the Author

This story came out of nowhere for me. I enjoyed writing it because sometimes it got a little crazy, but never unbelievable. Because crazy things do happen. It's how we bounce back from those things that happen to us (and around us) that inevitably will form us. Can we handle feeling out of control? Should we stay in unhealthy relationships? And how do we cope with great loss in our lives?

When I write a story, my hope is for my readers to feel the emotion and relate to the characters — just as I do. You may or may not have understood Beth's ultimate choice, but her desperation for something/someone was probably relatable. I hope you comfortably fell into the strong-bonded friendship between Tabitha and Carrie because you have been there in your life and you know there are fewer gifts more special than a tried and true friend. And when heartbreak led Carrie to begin a new path in her life, I hope you rooted for her because as we all know change and growth are not always easy to face.

From the Edge is my 17th published novel. I do hope this journey with all of you, my loyal and encouraging readers, continues for a very long time.

As always, thank you for reading!

love,
Lori Bell